Child
W to the
aters

Child to the Waters

James Everett Kibler

PELICAN PUBLISHING COMPANY
Gretna 2003

*The word "Pelican" and the depiction of a pelican are trademarks
of Pelican Publishing Company, Inc., and are registered
in the U.S. Patent and Trademark Office.*

Library of Congress Cataloging-in-Publication Data

Kibler, James E.
　Child to the waters / James Everett Kibler.
　　p. cm.
　ISBN 1-58980-095-8 (alk. paper)
　1. Southern States—Social life and customs—Fiction. 2.
Celts—Folklore—Fiction.　I. Title.
　PS3611.I26 C48 2003
　813'.54—dc21
2002012063

Printed in the United States of America

Published by Pelican Publishing Company, Inc.
1000 Burmaster Street, Gretna, Louisiana 70053

To my Connelly kin

We tell stories and listen to them as we listen to the coursing of water. —Russell Scott Sanders

Contents

Child
to the
Waters

Prelude
The Wild Bees of Truth

This is the country we return to
When for a moment, we forget ourselves. —Fred Chappell

Our storyteller has decreed that, here, the rules that govern the modern mind, so rigidly shaped by reductive science, neither guide nor apply. His is a land of voices sleeping deep in the blood, awaking in sleep and in dream, a realm of contraries where empirical limits are defined for the diminishments they are, then transcended triumphantly—a territory of known and remembered places, where the wanderer finds anchor and grows branches to stars. It is a place where the familiar roof tree sends its roots deep to bedrock and the sources of springs, declaring, "I will not be moved." It is a headwater place retrieved when the self is forgotten and goes free from its cell.

Our bard is a lover of the unseen. In his country, ambiguity can rest easily at the hearth. Here it is faith limited to the laboratory that is misshapen and out of place. The impoverishment of no belief is the rightful stranger here, having no seat in the communal ring at the fire. Our bard's realm is thus a joyful land of manifold richness, where the spirit holds absolute sway. Here, careerists do not climb our mossy, high crags; no nomad seeks in

11

ever-widening circles for power and gold. It has long been a fact that gold in the sun is far brighter than gold in the tomb of a bank's vaulted dark cells, and that stars seen of a winter cold night through bare limbs of the roof tree of home are far brighter than stars on a chart on a digital screen, or the silver of thirty strewn coins, thrown in the pitch-black of night.

These tales came as pure golden gifts, rounder and brighter than coins. They made their own way, sometimes from a glittering image, sometimes from memory of phrase or jagged sharp word. Their paths unfolded with glistening words from the pen like a river on page. They yielded themselves by turns of the mind—shining gift at each bend—as the teller's own journey was inspired on its way. They have found out their preordained ends like a river to sea. As we follow the windings and twists, our feet on sun-dapples that move and dance in the shade, or our eye on the waves neath our gaze, we follow the cadence of our gentle bard's voice, making its turns, translating dim, distant voices to words. As our guides are the wild bees of the way, lining to truth in the deep sanctum of woods, we follow down paths through misty green glens, trailing the still shining words, following by river's own shadowy banks and its eddying pools, through asphodel meadows to base of the moss-covered crag where the honey is stored. The bees may be wild but they visit our clover in our fathers' own fields, and hive in their bright golden cells not far from our very house door. And the journey is easy, led by hand of a child, and often attended by winds that arise in the path, and spin new-fallen leaves in great burnished swirls. These burst open gates of the pearl and the horn and turn dream into waking, and vision of night to the dazzling light of the day.

All stories are one, as all rivers are one. They shape from spring sources, and the fogs and the fens, the shining gold legends of place and of time, in winding continuous like river's own sure certain flow, and make transcendent full memory, carried as whispers deep from the blood, to arise then as gifts from a dream.

They are ritual and ballad, song and the dance. They cut deeper than razor-sharp edge of the voice, and are real as a rhythm is real, or a cadence, a heartbeat, a breath, or a rhyme. They rise from the great ancient cauldron of riddling old tales, that must always dictate their own special form. The stirrer must add and must stir, but mostly stand back from the smoke and the fire, and the bubbles that spatter and burst. The hearer must hear near the circle of fire, must draw close as he can, to catch every word, his back to the cold, but must also be cautious of sparks that would burn.

Then at last to the feast, he is welcome—and with food in abundance, and joy in the light and the warmth and the dance and the song, he can join in the ritual of sharing this meal in the cold desert night by tents of the wanderers there, a gift that like honey in heart of the stone will always be there to sustain.

Beneath desert stars, as they circle and turn, the smoke from the fire in the still of the icy dark sky makes a column to arise arrow-straight up above, around which the transient known world of illusion now centers and wheels in a jumble and dizzying blur. The heavens turn round at the ruby fixed point of a fire. Here at improvised hearth on the shifting dry sands of a chill desert night, our column of far-rising smoke extends, translates, and transforms, to a star-crusted roof tree of life. And a river of memory wells up *from the dried river-bed to whisper distinctly the ghosts of its waves. Listen. It speaks in the swirl of a new-risen wind.*

I

The Night Her Portrait Sang

. . . for our feet would linger where beauty has lived its life of sorrow to make us understand that it is not of the world. —William Butler Yeats

The ancient deep river ran noiselessly in its bed in the silent valley below, as candle glow on prisms in the great hall of the noble old house threw rainbow colors on the greying wall. The girandoles on the high dark mantel had an unusual glow about them, as light played from the paired gilt figures at candlesticks' base, from their features of face and folds of drape. Romeo's cape flared, and Juliet, in jeweled gown that flowed, leaned gilded shining face and breast to his. It was dusk into dark and no sound came.

The candles pointed heavenward from their pressed-glass bobèches, clotted with the fall and drip of beeswax the color of straw, their light as blonde as the hair on Juliet's brow. Flames did not dance. No breath stirred. The candles burned straight upward like cylinders, columns of glass. They had long since ceased to gutter and spew.

The dark from the old wavy panes of the windows settled down into ebony squares, and the candlelight lit their surfaces grey and opalescent from within. Shadows grew vertical, long, and still no movement or sound. Dust motes in air hung suspended and charmed, a levitation awaiting auspicious, august event, as if holding the breath, anticipating in time. It was the still of ancient marble obelisks, of hushed and glassy-deep, rush-lined pools, of gold-encrusted antique crowns, or carven ivory, or statues in stone, in a world growing vertical above the suspended, over the supine.

The child lay ill in the room upstairs, watched by an anxious old crone. Its frail fever-drained body was white as the linen whereon it reclined. Da's own face was so black it had a sheen of the radiant blue like the windows downstairs, or the blue clay her grandchildren dug to freshen her own cabin's hearthstone. The light from the hearth, in front of her now, made mirror in the sheen of her skin. Smoke rose from the tall house chimney in a column made pearl luminescent by winter's full moon, to hold up the roof of the heavens like a giant tent-pole. Around it and the great ancient tree at chimney's own side, the tapestry of sky circled and dipped, centered and spun, while the tree as if in mirrored reflection of the slow rising smoke sank its roots deeper in clay and the stone.

The child did not cry or stir. Its breath came shorter and shorter, slower and slower, weaker and weaker, as life slipped away. Da's mistress sat slumped into silence by the big poster bed, her rocking now frozen beneath frosts of her slumber like the dark fallow fields lying outside. Her head rested against one of the bedposts, whose carved sharp finials swirl-pointed on high. The vigil was long and the days now joined with the nights. Nights blurred into day.

Childbirth and fever had taken the little babe's mother just two nights before, and all in the house now mourned in the presence of death.

The woman in the rocker was called by the name of Miss Julia, whose granddaughter this was, sick in the cradle at kind old Da's knee. It was Julia's own precious daughter who died days ago. She mourned in her sleep, so exhausted was she in her body and soul.

Da likewise dozed and the world fell still: the sad little babe with her life ebbing ever so slow, the sad old woman feeling her loss through her sleep, the sad ancient nurse dipping her head in nods of sorrows and too many deaths. Her nose touched her chin in sharp outline of age and of grief.

The crystal tinkle and jangle of girandole prisms in the parlor below was heard by none. Nor seen were the particolored reflections of prisms exploded on the wall, or elongated shadows that moved as the candle flames thawed, shook themselves out, and danced. The dust motes scattered and whirled like leaves in a storm. Someone had passed, but none there saw. Beeswax sputtered to say; the candles guttered their words and intent. Wind from down the giant chimney blew smoke in the room in a circling swirl and crackle of ruby-bright coals. A momentous visitor this, and witness only the dark.

Up the polished walnut stairs now, the long silks trailed. The whispers of skirts against wainscot and wall came in the marble of silence. The house held its breath, as the babe's respiration slowed, and slowed.

Da sat up, eyes bright and round with waking. Miss Julia she roused with a word. Both heard it, the rustling of silks at the door, the whisper of satin, the current of air, and the flare-up of fire. And the babe, she was gone now, her breath ceased entire. Cold chill of the night and the grief settled in, in the dead chill of loss.

The mother had come for her babe, Julia knew. Da knew it as well, and they both kept their peace in a silence like death. Neither spoke nor got up, but waited in time for the something they knew must as talisman come as a sign. And came then it did, from below, in the strains that they knew, that they long loved familiar in life, and craved the sweet hearing again. On the radiant likeness of daughter caught on canvas in beauty of prime of her life, color came once again to her fingertips, shone on her cheeks, and on flush of her throat, as canvas then pulsed and lips grew vibrantly red like the bouquet of roses she held in her hand, lips that then blossomed to song. Julia heard the sweet voice of her daughter in the tune she had taught her as child, now translated to rhyme of a song and a story unheard by mortal before. The music had magic to soothe and sustain. It unlocked all the tears she had as yet been unable to cry. There the two sat, both silently crying, in rivers of cleansing, clear-flowing grief, like the untrammeled great river below.

Golden Romeo leaned again to his golden star-crossed mate, and the dancing candle flames settled back to their quiet and still. The last note from the red canvas lips quavered out, echoed long, then silent fell, as the candles sputtered, then guttered and spewed, flickered one last golden time, burned down, and then out, as meteors flared through the roof tree's bare branches and lit for bright moment the sky over grieving, winter dark fields.

II
Da

Da had progeny of her own. She sat often by the winter hearth thinking back on her children and the trials and tribulations she had in their raising. "I has sho been through lots of tight places," she mused.

No child tried her more than her eldest gal, Addie-Mae. At fifteen, she married Jim-Jesse Sims and moved seven miles, cross creeks and a river and trestle, to his own cabin home. It was when Addie-Mae's first babe was still sucking that Jim sent word that Addie was gone plumb crazy. She raved and flailed her arms about when they tried to get her to let her babe nurse. Addie had been going downhill two months before the child was born; and now a month old, the babe and its mama were both like to starve. Jim got so full of worryment that he too fell off, so that his skin lay real close to his bones. Da later found that poor Addie-Mae had had typhus and a sky-high fever that muddled her brain; but then they were perplexed, and Jim-Jesse called for her ma, not knowing what else he could do.

So Da left her good husband, Dave, to care for their children as best as he could between his farm labors and chores. The cabin was gloomy without her, and the children were fretting. The fire did not seem to burn as merrily at the hearth where her old empty rocker sat still and seemed to speak aloud that Da was not there. The children's crying eyes went unwashed, their clothes hung crooked, and they didn't eat right, but Da had to stay with her troubled child, who needed her most.

Addie-Mae screamed and flailed and, with her strong young body, was a handful for both Jim-Jesse and herself. At times they had to tie her down. Da took to switching her—"frailing the daylights out of her," as she clearly recalled. But Addie-Mae did not respond. Only exhaustion quieted her enough to let her poor baby suck.

The white doctor came and brought a bottle and some powders to mix with goat's and cow's milk. And the little boy thrived, but Addie herself only grew worse. Switching had done no good, nor her ma's commands. She could not be calmed. The fever had harmed her brain in earnest. One day she had gotten loose and run down the road with next to no clothes on, running to the river to drown herself, they feared. The neighbors, unsettled by her screams in the night, sent for papers at the courthouse to take her away.

Da and Jim-Jesse were distraught. They worried and puzzled but could find no way to quiet or comfort at all. Indeed, they tried everything, but fever came high and they knew she would die before they'd have to worry about the papers that would come to take her away. "Which would be worse than the other?" they asked.

And the raving got worse, so old Doc gave Da a bottle and rag. Da poured out of the bottle onto the cloth and waved it over Addie-Mae's face. She got stupid then, quieted, and slept. When after long hours she awoke, she asked her ma weakly and real low for a tumbler of water, and she calmed. For that day, the fever had broken and gone, at least for a time.

Then Da soon learned from Doc to ice Addie down. It took fifteen pounds to make an ice blanket, but it brought down the fever and quieted the fits. Then old Doc went to the neighbors. "Never mind the papers," he said. "All will be well." And Da and Jim-Jesse were at last relieved.

A few times when none of their nursing worked, Da sent Jim-Jesse for old Doc and he put a needle under her skin that settled the score and she slept. Please Doc, Da would beg, bring the needle again, and he did. For more than a week, every time the doctor came, he shot the medicine in her, and she stayed quiet and lay in the bed. Before that, Addie would abuse them all when she saw Doc coming, and flail and holler; but after he shot the stuff under her skin, all was quiet and she never abused them more. Addie-Mae took her medicine, and Da threw her switches away.

It seemed like years before Addie-Mae got better, but better she got. No, the papers for the asylum were not needed; and now only the medicine that old Doc prescribed was all that was required to keep her in line. Jim-Jesse went to his fields, a-plowing them straight, and Da gave Addie-Mae the thick white spoonful around the clock, in the day while Jim-Jesse worked and through the night while he slept and snored. Precisely at twelve, she would wake bolt upright and give her her spoon, and Jim-Jesse would snore. At four, she would wake and feed her her spoon, and Jim-Jesse would snore. "Mens ain't what they used to be no how," she would mumble. Sons-in-law most particularly.

Now many years hence, on this long winter's night before the hearth, she could say to Miss Julia with justifiable pride, "Addie-Mae ain't been to no 'sylum to this day and that baby done growed up strong and got babies grown of his own. Addie had six chilren after that, but never no more such strange goins-on in her head. If Doc and Jim-Jesse and us hadn't come along when us did, I 'spec Addie-Mae would a-gone to the 'sylum or died right there." Truly, the doctor had allowed that if it hadn't been for Da, they would have sure enough lost Addie-Mae; and that Da gave her her medicine better than any fancy city nurse—and her who had no book learning and could read nary a word.

Da stayed with her child three full months before she tried to go home to her Dave. She told old Doc she wanted to put her foots on her own doorsteps once more and to see her own little chilren. But Doc told her that Jim-Jesse had had enough and had been tried full sore, and if there was no one in the house to cook and clean, he was bound to light out over many rivers and never return. So Da stayed on two more months through the fall, missing her Dave and the children more and more.

Then at last the time came. Doc had dropped off coming to Addie-Mae's house, and Addie was going about on her own and was back strong enough to cook and do chores. So the Sunday arrived when Dave came to take Da home. "Home." The glorious word was enough to set her heart leaping.

It had been raining straight down for three whole days, and all the creeks and rivers were in flood. They had the seven-mile walk home through this, as final test and trial. At the railroad trestle, the water was shaking the cross-ties, and Dave had her by the hand pulling her along. She remembered his eyes about to start out of his head when she would stop every two steps and shout to the Lord to get her off of that thing. He allowed, "Come on here, Da. You ain't got no time to be stoppin' and prayin'. I left them chilren crying and alone, and now you is stopping every two steps to pray." Da recalled with a chuckle how she took her old umbrella and hit Dave spang a lick over his head, at which he dropped her hand and ceased to pull. "Lord God, Da, have you done gone out of your head like Addie?" he asked her, and Da recalled her answer complete: "I trusts in the Lord and I ain't letting no mortal man jerk me out'n my prayer."

All the rest of the way home, Dave spoke nary a word. He just trudged along with heavy boots in the water and mud, and chewed at his old pipe. Da had never hit him before, and it hurt his heart more than his head. She was that worn out from her half-year's trials with Addie-Mae, and that tired from the walk, and scared half to death from the trestle in flood. Her feet were lined with the accumulated cake of the red clay of her walk so as to make her near a foot taller. It was trudging so hard, and after so long. Trials, tribulations, and then some!

Finally, to break the long, pained silence, Da knew what to ask. "Dave," she intoned sweetly and slow with a drawl, "Dave, how is Mattie-Lou?" Mattie-Lou was their youngest, Dave's bright shining jewel and the joy of his life. With a tone of miff still in his voice, he allowed that she was crying when he left. Said Da: "Gwine make her and us all a big ash-cake on our hearth soon as I gets home and can." That's what it took, this message of their child and their home and hearth after so many months of being away. Dave perked up and acted more like himself from then on out. Dave had had his little misgivings at so long an absence and had wondered as any man would—and then to be struck on the head in that way. Yes, any mortal man would.

Da and Dave had to cross several swollen creeks on their way before they got home. It was dark and frosty and the children, all alone, were asleep in the open doorway, where they fell right down on the spot in the dark, looking anxiously toward Dave's return. Their eyes were wet and dirty from crying. Da had walked seven miles today, and Dave with his giant long stride had made fourteen. It had rained and rained, and the couple was tired and cold and wet to the skin. They picked up their young'uns and put them to bed without waking a one.

Yes, trials and tribulations, fever and flood, and old Dave now gone to his Maker above. The children grown up and all moved away. "Folks does do a heap for their chilren," she reflected to Miss Julia across a smoking cob pipe. "More than they'll ever think of doing for you." And then, like she remembered was the way of her son-in-law Jim, she fell easily into a low and soft, untroubled snore.

III
Dave

"If you caint serve your earthly pa, how is you ever gwine to serve your Heavenly one, I asks." So pondered Dave to Da. They had grown old together and the children were out on their own and too often forgot about them there in their little cabin on the edge of the big woods. The fire sent its curling cloud above the roof tree high to the stars as Dave puffed away at his pipe, making his own little column in rhythm with that of their hearth. Da had no reply. They both knew the truth of his claim.

Dave had been a good provider, considering the times, and raised their children well. His fields were clean of grass in summer, plowed fallow in winter, and manured in spring. He loved the life of the farmer and all that went with it—its sum total of sweat, toil, and triumph, its closeness to land.

Their little Mattie-Lou, the last to leave them, was married to a farmer too, and living the closest to home. He and Da, although slower now than in their prime, could walk the four short miles to her house, in less than a day. For the others, you needed a car; and that they did not have, could not afford, and did not want.

"The chilren travels fast in cars," he was wont to say. "But I just as lief to walk as to ride. Wrecks kills you off so quick you doesn't have time to repent. The chilren says we is ole-timey and don't know nothing 'bout living. Just the same, I likes slow movin', and takes mine out in walkin'." And Da agreed.

As Dave saw it, his sons and daughters were never at home. If he and Da made the long trek across the Tyger to Spartanburg or Greenville, the children would just as like not be there, but instead out joy-riding, going around in fast circles and getting nowhere. "As long as they have a quarter for gas," he said, "they're gwine to ride and come home broke."

"These fast ways makes sassy chilren," he would say to Da. "And sassy chilren that caint serve their ma and pa needn't think they can ride to the Promise Land in nary a automobile I ever seed. Ain't nobody got no business in automobiles 'cept lawyers, doctors, and fools."

His mule, ole Slim, was transportation fast and luxurious enough. Slim pulled the plow and could not be worn out with pulling a wagon or riding except in a crisis and pinch. So Slim and Dave were respectful friends. Dave talked to him in lieu of a son. He had not replaced Slim with the green and yellow usurper that belched clouds of soot, burned his nose with the smell of gasoline, and destroyed the peace of the day with its grate of steel grinding on steel.

"Yes. I takes my walkin' and my talkin' slow," Dave declared, and he and Da had long since fallen successfully into the easy cadence of the place—the cadence of the slow-moving seasons, the cadence that ole Slim followed as he pulled the shining and new-sharpened plow.

Da rocked in tune with the music of their conversation. The pauses in their talk punctuated the night, like refrains from old-time ballads, like the steady rhythmical creak and give of the rocker rung against well-worn wood.

One recent Sunday evening Da had been at a field near their house when a light little bird of an airplane with bright silken wings had touched down. Two men in goggles and scarves jumped out from a little door and people flocked and laughed and joked and frisked about. "Old woman," one of the men called. "Come on here and get you a ride. We'll take you up high." She had quickly declined with a toss of her head. "Right den and dar," she told Dave, "I allowed that when I goes up like dat, I sho ain't gwine up wid no man. I'se gwine up wid Jesus." And that was that, and Dave had approved.

On this long gentle night in her memory, Dave still gave final pronouncement as he had in his day: "Flying high and never gettin' nowhars seems to satisfy these chilren nowadays, so I don't know what is to become of them. They caint serve nothin' but theyselves." This was certainly no parting patriarchal blessing, and was said and remembered neither as benediction nor curse, but only observation keen, pure, profound, and sad with great loss. Where was the son to follow Dave's plow?

And their children's own children showed the results. "If you fools with cars, you ends up in jail," Dave solemnly declared. That was the simple equation more profound and certain than Einstein's own; and jail was disgrace. He had never been there, never lost his freedom to bars, locks, and walls, he was so proud to say. But several of the grandchildren had, for petty things enough and for short stays, but jail just the same. And still they were young.

"We lives in changing times, Da," he said to his wife of fifty years, and the grey of the smoke circled the grey of his head. A restless age, this new time. "Folks marry, then when the red gets off the candy, they divorce. Too much moving. Too much scouting around," old Dave had wisely observed. "As for me, I'm a local 'gator and ain't happy except in my own swamp. I'd rather be the porest red-bone hound at my cabin on the Tyger and bay at the moon than be the richest man in Spartanburg." His words came back to her as if it were just yesterday.

Da's own pipe had gone out, and the chill of dead embers before her brought her back to the night there at hand. Dave had been gone for many long years, and now it was Miss Julia who dozed at her side. She knocked out her pipe and rose stiffly one more time on her tired old bones, easing toward the goose-down of bed, and the comfort of quilts.

IV

Shone and the Whispering Bridge

Just as Shone came to the bend in the road that revealed the river below through an arch of thick trees, a little whirlwind played mischievously, miraculously, with last year's leaves straight ahead in his path. It danced right on by, and through its bright golden swirl, Shone could see that the yellow native fieldstone of the bridge's supports mirrored the precise tawny, rich color of the river in flood. Froth around the bases of these solid rock piers was the color of peaches and cream. So thought Shone, who was hungry, and grew hungrier still as he jostled along in the rhythm of wagon on this fine July day. Peaches were luscious and ripe in his father's own orchard, where they fell with the weight of their sweetness, overripe from the trees and circled by bees and droning red wasps drunk on their juice; his mind was on these, and getting home, and sitting down, with his feet out of the heavy wet clay-crusted boots and propped up on a chair, his mind free to wander and roam.

He had taken the wool to market and had made a good trade; and now in the wagon behind the roan stallion, he was heading for home and peaches and cream, and his new young wife, whose skin was softer than either the skin of a peach or the petals of pale damask rose, and sweeter and prettier than peaches and cream.

Deep in his breast pocket, he carried the pin he had bought at the store—a gold gyring circlet with the single round ruby like a small drop of crimson-bright blood. He loved buying her pretties and seeing the shine of her eyes in delight.

They had been married now for more than a year, and no babe on the way. He wondered at that, for it wasn't for the lack of their doing. He blushed at the thought of his old pals' off-color ribbing, and even his mama's and pa's. "Better get moving," Pa had said. "There's fallow fields to plow, and sons that's needed for plowing."

His mind had wandered down these shady paths again, where the willow trees lapped full and in folds of emerald green; but Shack soon brought him back to the sunlight of day as they came to the bridge's first wooden planks. It was here at what the folks of the place called the whispering bridge that Shack balked and stood still, and would in no sort of a way be cajoled to put horseshoe on wood. Had old Shack heard the stories that were told of this place? His ears pricked up and stood at alert, while his hide quivered all over as though sheep-flies were stinging severe. The horse was not hard to please, and had never given trouble this way before. So Shone was wondering too. Animals always could tell if haints were about long before men—or was it the whirlwind of leaves they'd just passed, or more likely the water in uneasy swirl through the cracks of the bridge? It did look right strange to come out of a whirlwind and next minute be walking on water below. Shone put all the thoughts of a haint far aside. Besides it was in the bright light of the day.

"Come up, Shack. Move your lazy tail, old fellow," he proclaimed in his low gentle drawl, somewhat more loudly than was his wont. "It's home we're headed, and for hay and for stalls and for peaches and cream."

But Shack would not heed, nor budge, nor stir. Stubborn as the proverbial mule, he was; but he was a horse, and a fine high-strung young blood in his day, sire of many young foals on the place.

A pull on the bridle, a tug at the reins, and Shack finally gave way. Shone mounted the wagon again, settled still in his seat as the bridge scaffolding began to flow past in its usual motion and play.

It was an old covered bridge, high on sturdy stone piers, but creaky decrepit with age, pine boards warped, cedar shakes on its roof patchy askew, letting squares and diamonds of sunlight inside. Through the holes, the sun played in a dance on Shone's face with its rays.

The bridge sighed and groaned like a moaning old man as the two made their way, and Shone's wagon wheels now rumbled hollow on wood.

About two-thirds across, Shack froze in his tracks once again, and this time for certain to stay. His ears stood alert and a-quiver like before, as if listening to song.

Shone heard it too this time, and then again faint as song of a siren to Odysseus at sea, or of maidens on Lorelei rock far away. It came as a whisper, then song, then a sigh, and a sob. "Just the water in swirl, Shack. Let's get on our way." He dismounted the wagon and pulled, but heard it again. Frail whisper like faraway cry of a child, it came once again, and lower this time but distinct as the tones of his wife calling him in from the fields for the day, to the supper she'd fixed with loving soft hands.

"Mercy, mercy, and save, please save," it prayed. It begged and it pled, "Save. Save. Mercy. Please save." He must get gone from the bridge and out of this day. He'd crossed the path of a haint, and in full light of the day! He pulled at old Shack, who responded at last; and he placed boot on the footboard to rise and quickly go on.

It was then that he saw the hand of the child through cracks of the floor. Its white little fingers had caught to the roots of a big black crag far below that had washed down in the flood and lodged between two of the piers. Caught there in swirl, the child was very far gone, too exhausted to do more than hold and say *Save.* Shone was close enough to see his gentle sad eyes looking up in the pleading of need and distress to his own. A flesh and blood child, not the mist and ghost of a dream.

It was far down the bank and Shack to pull, the rope

tied to Shack and Shone and saving the boy. His thin little body shivered and shook. Cold and white as marble or snow was the tiny lad's skin. His color, it came and it went, ebbed with his breath, then came once again as Shone rubbed warmth in his limbs and at last blew hot breath in his chest. He slept then at last in Shone's burly great arms.

Peaches and Shone had a little lost child, a gift from the flood, lost from a couple who'd been swept from their wagon and drowned at a crossing upstream. Shone and Peaches never had more babes of their own. Learned physicians may could have said why, but God's voice was enough. This is the way it was meant. And as simple as that.

The little child of the flood from the whispering bridge grew tall and still taller, and tawny of limb and of hair, like the color of river's own wave in flood. He muscled the plow and sang deep from the chest of life and of love, of fiddles and furrows, and of peaches and cream. He bent to the fields like one born of the earth, and *to* it as well—a giant of sorts, pleasant of face, with broadest and frankest of smiles. Yet *not* born of the earth, but delivered of river in flood. And like waters that quickened and gave life to the soil, his sons they were many and his daughters were bounteous and joyful and fair, and like honey and peaches and cream for the sons of the land.

V

Sad Conacher at Gordon's Mill

The old grindstones were merry. They made meal, flour, and grits and never grew tired or needed a rest. The clack of the wheel and the rumble and clap of the stone, the creaking of wood and the rush of the trace, made as lively a sound as would come to the ear.

But Conacher, the miller, was down in the dumps this fair autumn morn and didn't know why. The best of times always brought sadness to him, and the saddest made him merry. He was made backwards that way, he said to himself, and made effort to change. But time after time, his attentions had all come to naught. Far easier to make red birds from blue, or a wren from a jay, than to turn Conacher's channel from its deep riverbed.

The farmers trooped in happy and stomped in their boots. The jokes that they cracked brought him faint little smiles, but no great belly laughs like he heard. Their songs, sung out lustily, never caused him to hum. The mill cat watched slyly as down Conacher would sit, his elbows on knees, and his long greying face on his hands. Through palest white lips, glum Conacher prayed for a change, but for days and then weeks, no change came.

Then one day when he was glummest and he least expected it, a great gurgle of water and violent splash in the trace brought him straight to his feet. A giant long fish somehow had got trapped in the trace. And that was the cause of commotion and all that transpired. It was a shining fat sturgeon, pert-near size of a man, that had knocked all the water clean out of the trace. There it lay, fins outspread like great silken wings. The mill wheel had stopped in midturn, and the grindstones had come to a halt in midgrind. The still in the air was as weird as could be, for mills, as you know, are the busiest and noisiest of the places of men.

A six-foot sturgeon suspended in midair on his trace as if it were in an invisible gold-threaded net! What a thing to behold! Man-sized fish that glowed like a rainbow and floated and hovered and flew. Conacher's face showed amazement, then a smile, and a laugh. The laughter shook loose like a dam that had broke, and he laughed till the tears got unlocked from his eyes. And down they all rolled in torrents like tawny great river below. He laughed and he laughed and the laughter rang out and bounced off of the rocks and echoed in glens, down valleys to meadows where the cows stopped chewing their cuds. "Old Conacher is unbridled happy," they registered amazed through their grass-fragrant drool. Old Bossy was frozen, green tuft in her mouth with a single white daisy hanging down from its long broken stem.

The bubbles in the river winked mischievous eyes at each other and grew round and popped in their glee. The cat was also amazed and let a plump mouse pass a few feet away. At which, when he had time and breath, the mouse too was amazed and started to laugh. This tickled the cat, who had never heard mouse laughter before, and she laughed and she laughed till she rolled on the floor in a soft golden ball.

No grain was ground that day. No flour, no cornmeal, no grits, no money was made. So Conacher went home to his wife in the middle of day, and when she got over the shock, she laughed when she saw him, so extraordinary it was. He was dutiful and sober, hardworking always, always on time and a penny to make and a penny to pay. No time off for him, either early or late.

But this day, his boys and his girls were now at his knee, and he told them the story, much to their glee. They laughed and they laughed as they took turns around, playing horse on his knee.

Having done its due that holy fine day, sturgeon wriggled its rainbow scales on its way to the river below, and fluttering its fins like great silken wings as if to wave "goodbye to y'all!" was off to the deep. In the middle of night, water flowed on the trace and over the wheel, and turned it again. In the light of the heavy great harvest moon, the stones ground their grain on their own. The farmers came in the next morn and, no sad miller around, deemed the mill a ghost-haunted mill, working with grace alone on its own, and gathered their own, and poured corn on the till, bagged flour and meal, and left coins on the chair, to be guarded by cat.

From then till this day, Conacher comes to the mill to get rent from the cat, who pays out the coins as cat wisdom decides, with the wiggle of whisker and wrinkle of smile. And Conacher can laugh till he cries, with his wife, and his children on knee, in the river's great fertile valley below.

VI
Quar

~◈~

Mazen Prysock slept in the shavings of his woodworking shop because his wife wouldn't 'low him inside. Now Mazen was a good furniture maker, known well and wide. He made tables and chairs, pie-safes and cupboards, bedsteads and stools, even wagons and more. If it could be turned and planed and doweled and hammered from wood, he could make it with skill. Even goat-carts for the children came from his hands, wagons in miniature, perfect and sure.

But Mazen was *quar,* as we country folk say. He was a mite bashful when meeting with women and men. He'd buy him a pair of new overhalls in each bird-hatching spring and never take them off until they were threadbare with wear. He wore a great leather belt over them tight at his waist. His galluses were red and tufted with sawdust and shavings of wood.

No doubt it was the having no baths that kept him from bed of his wife. So under the fragrant shavings of cedar and pine, like blankets and quilts, in his woodworking shop he would sleep. Through all the long winter, like some great unkempt bear, he hibernated alone.

It was wonder that he had wife a-tall. She would never be from among us, we all knew for sure. So he went over the river into the county next door where his ways weren't known, spent a week, brought her home, and we neighbors marveled and swore, "That ole Maze; he's a caution and more!"

And the new Missus was no beauty. In fact, the unkind among us said she was so ugly she could make an eight-day clock stop cold. Others declared she'd fallen out of the ugly tree and hit every limb on the way down.

Like Maze, his wife was *quar* too, as anyone linked to Maze must of necessity be. She let none of us inside her door. Or even through the gate. One evening the Cathcart women down the road came up through the woods with their children for a neighborly call. The Prysocks had an old wheezing organ that the Missus brought with her from home when she got married to Maze. This they had seen and remembered although they'd never heard it played there before.

One of the young'uns wanted to play on the organ, because she knew how and had none but this one around. (She had learned in the town.) They stood at the gate with their hands in their shawls. The little wooden house was surrounded by circular fence of the native honey-colored fieldstone. The gate, it was fastened and the Missus was curt: "If y'all want in the yard, you will have to climb over the fence."

This, ladies in skirts and shawls did not do, so they left with the tale that Missus Prysock was *quar*—like her husband was *quar*. Hollyhocks of palest soft pink bloomed at the gate and were never disturbed. The mosses grew thick and were not cleared away.

"Ole Missus Prysock wouldn't give you air in a jug," we mumbled and grumbled around. But none of us ever went back. What charity she had, started and ended at home. And as for ole Maze, he never saw mortal to seek it, much less dole it out. His peddler's wagon went out twice a year full up with his wares of fragrant new wood, and he sold and returned. They kept to themselves and were talked of around and were left to be *quar*. "*Be* that way, then!" 'twas said by us neighbors with shrug of the shoulders and many a hand on the hip.

Then when they were old, ole Maze and the Missus had a child. That was the *quarest* of all. The tales went around that it must have been got between pairs of overhalls, or more likely was carved outen chinaberry wood and conjured to life. Many a knee was slapped, and many the guffaw. But mostly we all just scratched our heads and tried to make sense of it all.

The babe, a gal child, was the prettiest young'un that any had seen. Her body was honey colored like a golden wood's orchid or the new-flowered magnolia with the sunlight behind. Only her cheeks and throat and fingertips flushed with the blush of the dooryard's hollyhock. Her hair was the jet of lampblack and ravens shining in sun, her eyes clearest blue as the larkspur, or wild gentian flower.

They named her Deirdre, there in the woods, a name not any about had heard ever before. "Deirdre?" we neighbors questioned. "Deirdre!" we intoned. "Deirdre," we droned. "Deirdre," we mumbled. "Deirdre," we grumbled and groaned. "Deirdre! How *quar,* like Missus and Mate!" Name suited the scene, there in the little old unpainted house with its circling stone fence in the clearing of solitary wood, like something straight out of a fairy-tale book.

No matter the talk. Little Deirdre was the joy of an old man's late life. And her baby fingers curled about his own like the fragrant pine and cedarwood that came in curls from his plane.

She played in the shavings with her toys made of wood. The floor it was littered so thick with rabbits and carts, and cats and ducks, and wheels and dolls, and goats and horses, sheep and such, that Maze had to dance to keep from spoiling them as he walked to and fro at his work.

"Deirdy," he called her. The joy of his life.

Deirdre and Maze were inseparable friends. She often slept in her own little pile of his shavings near his, and she hummed as he turned out the spindle of wood on his lathe. She wove music of lathe into music of song.

But no change did she make in the way Maze and his wife went about, or, more accurately, did not. The hollyhocks still grew undisturbed at the unopened gate. The moss grew even more emerald lush and velvet by the stones of the door. No stranger's own shadow touched threshold of floor. Maze still bought his overhalls each early spring at the store, and he slept in the shavings of his tidy shop floor.

But the sound of the organ now often came from house windows and door. The neighbors crossing down the lanes to and fro marveled at the sound of old ballads from deep in the woods, and of music the likes they'd not ever imagined before. Her voice was as clear as the thrush and as winning as her eyes were gentian blue. Deirdre was growing a woman, and her beauty grew great in like store.

"Pretty babes make ugly grownups" was an old local saw. Over many known cases, which proved the saying true, many a knee was slapped and came many a broad guffaw. But Deirdre proved the saying wrong *squar*—as *squar* as the Prysocks were *quar.* Nothing in fact was ever usual with Prysocks, and Deirdre, most certain of all. On the occasions she had been seen tending the flowers in the Prysock garden and yard, her smile was never forgotten and was talked of around as deeply as in the past the Prysocks had been talked of as *quar.*

She positively took the breath away. A single glance caused catch in the throat, and neighboring tongues for once held their peace. There was just no explaining, no putting all this into words. Legend might only achieve it, and only with time—and after our riddling to sort some of it out, if ever we could. Though we accepted, it mystified all. The most beautiful mortal that had ever graced our common old soil with her light-footed trod. Her movements were like we imagined a swan on the wave, or the distant deer we knew on the hill. She fired the imagination with a look or gesture that gave meaning to all common things. Seen from afar, let her kneel and stroke the head of a fine hunting dog and you felt that there was good in all things.

She played on the old organ in strains of her own. She made trances of song and wove charm of her tunes. They glowed like her smile and her eyes and her shining dark hair. Both her heart and skill grew strong and as one, and revealed their quality in her body that blossomed like the great laurel tree.

And what was so odd, although cheerful her voice and joyful her lot, the songs that she sang had the saddest refrain. They had sadness married inside of joy, and the joyous in midst of the sad. A melancholy there was in the heart of her cheer, like all natures of creatures that grow up alone in the wood and trained most deeply in nature's sure ways. As she sang, it appeared she looked deep to another world, as if just outside the light of her window or half-open door.

This evening she sang her dear sweetest best. The first was a ballad of leaving a home and the homesickness that would come:

In the bright sunny South in peace and content,
Oh, the days of my childhood I scarcely have spent,
From the deep flowing spring to the broad flowing stream
Ever dear is my memory. How sweet is my dream.
I leave my confinement and comfort alike,
For the dangers of fortune, privation, and strife . . .

The sad strains came in snatches to the ear in the shifts of the breeze:

> *Oh my father looked sad as he bid me to part,*
> *And my mother embraced me with anguish of heart,*
> *And my kind gentle brother looked paled in his woe,*
> *As he hugged me and blessed me and bid me to go.*

And then lines from another old tune drifted to passers-by:

> *Youth will in time decay, Eileen Aroon.*
> *Beauty must fade away, Eileen Aroon.*
> *Castles are sacked in war;*
> *Chieftains are scattered far.*
> *Truth is a fixed star,*
> *Eileen Aroon.*

As for Maze, he'd become now a very old man, with face as wrinkled as a winter apple. He had grown a mite deaf, but he still leaned and harkened to his fond Deirdy's song. The trance of her song put all his deep questions and fears and riddles aside. That was the magic of Deirdre, who accepted all life with her innocent faith.

Those in her presence, she calmed, and all in the earth took on joy of her beauty perfected and charmed. In intricate pattern, she taught Maze the paths of her song and her harmony's way, and even as death had approached him, he never feared more. The circle of life formed him charmed, and when he must quit it, he'd just be a part of the charm. Deirdre's song for him raised all the leaves of the wood into language, and brought the wild creatures to stillness and sighs.

And from the time she could toddle to walk in the wood, Maze had taught, and still taught her, *his* paths, intricate like her song, in the maze of the trees. The cherry and walnut, the elder and holly and ash, he would seek them all out, would cut them and carry them home. Before taking a piece, he would talk to the branch or the trunk and ask its permission—would seek its reply. Ofttimes he would pass, leaving the tree or the branch untouched and unharmed. For these paths in the woods would be Deirdre's to walk when time took him away, and those trees left behind would be Deirdre's old friends to be asked in their turn.

He taught her his lore of the woods, held back not a jot of his treasure of wisdom, or word-horde of his riddling old tales. The flora and fauna alike made his lore. He taught her hourly, day after day, and instinctively, constantly, as breath and the beat of the heart. At night in the sky, he taught her the stars and their stories, and well she had learned all the things that he said. Of their wheelings and circling, returning—all went in her song. No towns had she seen, neither grate nor rush of machines, nor fads and throngs of the day. No jangle of discord, to cause her to weep and dismay.

One day in the wood, old Cathcart, the nearest neighbor, heard old Maze and his Deirdre out asking a tree. He shook startled his head, refusing to credit his ears. He shook head and shook, and concluded that Maze with his ripest old age was now *quarer* become. And now as for that beautiful child, she was destined to be that *quar* too.

The talk got around of Mazen's talking to trees, and even authorities official were consulted a time or a two. *Lame-brained* was the phrase bandied around. Nothing came of it, sure, for all of us had known the family had right to be true each to each. And if it came to a crisis, we'd pitch in to help, if help we'd then be allowed. So the talk stayed mainly just talk and we neighbors wagged tongues and shook heads and would say, "That Maze is a caution. He's now talking to trees."

He now was also our puzzle and riddle at once; we could figure and cypher and muddle our heads and come up empty and short. And that, it was that. No bother beside. Gathered in, like a lark to its mate in the nest, we took the *quar* Prysocks inside.

As for Deirdre, she had now learned all stock and store of ole Mazen's legends and tales, deep lore of the wild-woods, flowers and fields, rivers and skies. Her talent at song had blossomed like the great golden rose at their door, and he taught her his songs, her mama taught her hers, the mockingbird even lent her his airs, and Deirdre invented her own magical tunes.

Mazen's time-seasoned fiddle he continued to polish with many an elbowing bow, and well had she learned this also. The organ and fiddle made music so wondrous that the neighbors who passed in the wood would sit rapt in their wagons or freeze still on their feet, to listen for long and still long, and then listen some more. From this harmony pure, we knew ole Mazen was good in his soul, and though family's heart was pure *quar,* was sound and okay. We left them in peace and grew joyous ourselves to have them in midst. Some puzzles must stay, and be riddled for aye. It redounded to bless all the neighbors in blessing unfolding and doubling as day led to day. It was comforting sure to have our *quar* Prysocks at song in the wood.

And this was the *quarest* of all. To strangers, we *boasted* of decrepit, ancient ole Maze and his wife and their beautiful gal. The most wondrous of all—our rhyme was uncertain until Mazen's own fiddle would call, or left cut clean in two, till supplied back as whole through echoes of Deirdre's own tune—the song of her singing, invention, and skill.

There was content and peace in our pastures, and on all our joyous larkspur-blue hills. We longed never to leave. The river flowed on smoothly and surely in its deep carven banks, and would sing only the songs of Deirdre's devising and will. For all came to know, it was those that the great river loved best, sung by its own, grown from its own, a melody rising sublimely from out of the joy and content of the common old soil of the place—the most beautiful words of the most beautiful of the daughters of men—the grace of the innocent blessed, given beyond understanding and all our deserving, for just no clear reason a-tall.

VII
Singin' Billy, the Song Catcher

. . . sweet fields array'd in living green
And rivers of delight. —William Walker, *Southern Harmony*

When a redbird perched on her little Billy's cradle and sang and sang with full-throated ease, his mama should have known he'd grow up to have the fullest music inside. The rocks of his cradle and the hum of her voice, tracing the paths of tunes caught in her memory, sunk themselves deep, deep in his own baby mind, and cut like the wagon roads growing deeper through his green valley home, made from the passing of many a wheel. The wheels' own tunes were music in their dry creak and clack. Little Billy watched and listened to the rhythm of heavy-packed wagons, groaning and laboring, then speeding free on their way. They were filled to the brim with chestnuts and apples, tobacco and such, out from the misty cold coves of the mountains, out of the valleys and hillsides of far miles away, heading steep down our paths to the great shining sea.

Or else the wagons sheltered people, making their way to new fertile lands, the women wide-eyed in bonnets, the men stalwart and serious, walking or riding bright roans and shining bays beside, whistling and singing their oldest of songs. The wagons clanked with dangling lanterns, and cookpots and tins, as a few cattle labored behind, clip-clopping close behind them in tether, lowing and chewing, swinging their tails that beat time as they flicked off the greenbottle flies.

All this music of motion got caught up with the music of birds, the swaying of trees, the sound of the wind in the pines, the flow of the river, and his mother's low hum, Southern harmonies all.

She sang the old songs, remembered from her mama before, as she sat as a girl at her own mama's knee. These songs crossed an ocean in the cleaving sharp keels of great ships and carried their rhythms through salt-spray and heaves of the storm. The waves got mixed up in the tunes and altered their tone, but the rhythm remained.

They began in the wet, bright greens of moss-covered mounds on Meath's broad brow and Armagh's hills. They carried the magic of pipes and harps, of jigging reels, and the sídhe—the longing of blue crags and Tara's misty far dells. She sang now their music, and Billy, he listened deep, long and long.

Ma and Pa carried him right from the start to Lower Fairforest Church. He lay cradled in cleft of his mama's warm arms as he heard, and drank deep of the sounds, as he suckled in time at the breast. They were lining the tunes; and the clapboarded building itself echoed like hollow wood body of wagon or ship, like the hollow of guitar or fiddle, the meeting house trembling and singing like the walls of a great calling drum. The planks and beams from the ancient timbers sang with the voice of the giant old trees, cleared away to make churches and cabins and wagons and ships, then guitars and fiddles besides. The song leader, he had a strong studhorse of a voice, that pulled all the people, like wagon or plow, and leaving its wake in the pleasure of motion and brightness of seeded and new-risen crops. He swayed as he sang and they swayed as they followed behind. As baby, Billy rocked there in cradle that lived and that breathed.

As Billy grew older and could ramble the woods on his own, he soon found the banks of the Tyger, where he sat long and long, or rippled its waves with the skipping of stones.

The circular wakes of the stones on the grey were ballads themselves, frozen to sight, with rhythms out-casting to reach far away. The lapping of waves on the banks caused young Billy to nod and to sway, would sing him to sleep in a bug-humming, high summer's noon.

The stars had their rhythm on clear winters' nights as he watched their bold wheel in a dance majestic and epic in scope. They could not be altered, rearranged by a whit, or hurried a jot, but kept their own paths like the roads of the wagons, cut by sharpest of wheels on the floor of his valley below.

And the motion of seasons would not change rhythm a jot. This he sensed and then learned, as he grew a strong lad, and stood with legs wide and feet planted firmly on the furrows he'd plowed.

As he walked on his way, shoe-soles made their own tune on the summer's hard clay. As older he grew, the gait of his steed and the roll of her jog grew a part of his flesh like the pulse of his heart or the quickening drawing of breath.

Late in the night, as he pondered the world and its unmeasured ways, he watched the distant and icy-cold stars and listened to the taking of breath or beat of blood in his veins—mysteries far off and inside at one time and the same, deep to the core and high as the sky. He heard still the same from his brothers, who lay close beside his own trundle bed, or the bass of his pa's stentorian snore from the room next to theirs. Like the meeting house walls, the walls of their home resounded with rhythms to make their own tunes. They sang all the same, one song complete of the rhythm of life.

His legs, they grew steady, strong, and stout from the plow, his limbs supple from swimming strong Tyger's wave. They refined in the dance, of the circling of reels and the fancy abandon of soloing jig. His feet joined the rhythms of furrow to floor, a dance of the soil mated to dances on new-cut resinous sweet-smelling pine. The floorboards themselves sang with voice of the primeval wood, the old forest pristine whose spirit was ever still there. And the rhythm of feet and the blood, as he watched the far stars, now met in the rhythm of eyes touching each. A pair of bright eyes in the dance had brought him to center and now caused his own to line in a rhythm mirroring hers.

Her name was Amy Golightly, and dance lightly she did. She was Eve to his Adam in an Eden's fair land. He added his rhythm to hers and they danced soon as partners, paired off from the world but mirroring dances of all, and from times long before, and to come.

Well, Billy, like Adam, grew strong by his Eve, and they added the rhythm of babes of their own, whose bounces on knee made music and harmony their own; and he sang them old harmonies he'd learned at his own mama's knee, from her mama before. Amy did same, and husband and wife sang to each.

And this is true story of Tyger's own son, our own Billy Walker, "Singin' Billy" he's called. He caught up the songs and passed them on down through his books and his own singing schools. He walked and he rode and beat time with the clip-clop of hooves for many a year—songs living in flesh and the brain and their tunes in his gait. They came from the place as our own Billy did. Now we sing him today like the voice of the old vanished forest, rhythms of stars, or the motion of seasons, like the blood in our veins or the rock of the cradle or music of bird, that first perched on his cradle as sign of the things all to come.

VIII
A Perfect Day for Tyger Fish

*If you are ever going to be at home, you must know and honour
the local powers, and nothing is more steadily, undeniably
powerful than the river .* —Russell Scott Sanders

Their granny had woven good, sturdy fish traps from
the pliable strips of white oak. The curls from their father's
drawing knife had come long and thin as a master's gift.
Then with the strips of wood, they and Granny had creat-
ed long, deep, funnel-shaped cones of loose basket weave.
They shone white and slick in the yellow autumn noon like
great new Amalthea's horns.

"Let's run 'em on down," said Darcy-Joe to his brother
Nish.

As the two wound their way across the valley slopes to
the river, the maples and sassafras burned orange-scarlet as
fire coals under giant, arrow-straight tulip poplars growing
gold in the sun.

"If y'all drop and bust a one of these, I'll clean your
rabbits sure!" old Granny had warned as they went on their
way. And she meant it, they knew. Second to cleaning the
rabbits of little misbehaving young'uns, it was Granny's
chief duty to weave and work the oak into place. The men

would bring in the wood, would draw it into strips. Then she would fashion all of the baskets for the farm and the kitchen—cotton-picking baskets, wood-gathering baskets, corn-baskets, pea-baskets, blackberry-picking baskets, egg-shaped egg-baskets, and chair bottoms and backs, floor mats, and more, all from the serviceable oak. These fish traps were just toss-offs, but stout and well made, as were all of the gifts from her hands.

The boys fooled and played as they walked in the usual way of boys on a fishing great autumn day. Nish wore his basket over his head like a great pointy crown. He looked furtively, mischievously, out of the holes in its weave with his lash-heavy dark eyes.

Darcy-Joe, who was older and taller, carried two. With his arms poked inside, he wore his baskets as great bulbous sleeves, flapping them like the giant white-headed eagles that nested over their heads in ton-heavy nests on the high river crags. Remarkably, no mishaps occurred and the baskets all made it intact, thus saving the boys' rabbits a cleaning this time.

The Tyger was moving serene in a glow. Its tawny, rich waters had a slight cast of green. Its bubbles were as bright a yellow as the brothers' blonde hair, and the sun's reflection in the water glinted bright in the brothers' brown eyes.

"There's fiddle off the wall, and cornbread in the pan," Darcy-Joe hummed in an improvised song. "Build up the fire. Bank up the coals. The catfish are ready to jump in my plate and make me a meal." He danced a little clumsy jig as he looked at the river's far banks and the great poplar trees that rose high on its hill.

Darcy-Joe and Nish had to weight the fish traps down with stones. The catfish that they sought fed on the river's rich floor.

Darcy-Joe had a pail of chicken guts tied to his belt. This was the only grief and nuisance of the day. The bottle-green flies sometimes caught up to them, and hummed around, and bit and stung. This was the bait, and in loose burlap pouches, the guts were tied in the back of the cones. "Come and get it, you catfish!" Nish solemnly intoned, as the baskets made their splash on the wave.

Deep, deep, the cones sank as the river sang low of its life and its richness, unselfish provider to men.

The muscadines on river's edge were heavy with grapes. Wasps could be heard as they rattled and droned overhead on the overripe ooze of sweet juice. The boys ate them a few of the selectest ones easiest to reach, and cut loose a trio of vines that hung down to the water from tall river trees. These were all of the ties that were necessary to hold the trio of baskets in place, and provided the ropes to retrieve them when baskets were full. A matter of minutes saw the fish traps weighted, baited, sunk, and tied—ready to receive the grace of the crop of the deep. And they? They, even as boys, already stood ready, like their grownups before, with strong languid souls, to accept what the unseen depths of the great swollen river would bring. Their souls were like tough sturdy-made nets and the stout-hearted split-oaken traps—standing ready and open to wait and receive.

And the tawny old Tyger itself flowed on strong, languid, and long, while blonde-headed brothers horsed their way on back home, on up the autumn's colorful quilt-patch of hill.

As their eyes opened up to a sunny new day, the brothers dressed fast as they could in a glee. Granny straightened their belts and tucked in their tails, and yelled out open door as they fled, "If y'all young'uns drop ary one of them fish, I'll clean your rabbits sure!"

They horsed down the great valley trace, took time to tumble and dart, threw yellow fat walnuts to hit upside their heads like a rock. Rough, innocent play, and their fingers turned walnutty brown like their eyes. The great forest rang out with the sound of their joy.

Three fish baskets were there on their muscadine ropes just as they'd left them the previous day. They had hardest of times getting the first one up, so full it was against the great river's flow. They strained and strained, but they finally won and pulled it ashore. It was filled with its treasure of catfish so beautiful, shiny, and grey, that they laughed and rubbed bellies and laughed all around.

Their whiskers a-twiddle, the fish numbered ten. All were over foot long, and one huge old fellow measured three. A big mess of fish from just one basket alone!

The next basket held only four, but all big fine ones and a handful to bag. Into great croaker sacks they all went.

Not one got away. Then Darcy-Joe and Nish baited baskets and sank them again, then tied them with vines like before.

The third of the baskets was hardest of all to get out. It seemed to have life of its own; and when finally it did come up to the shore, astonishment shone from the two brothers' bigger brown eyes. For, instead of a catfish, was a fish from the Tyger they'd not ever seen. For once, they stood silent in place.

It was single fish only inside of the cone, and delighted the lads with its bright-colored scales that were brighter than moonlight on water, or light from ten dozen lamps. There was flash of the ruby and emerald's green. The topaz was seen as flecks in the midst of the clear sapphire's blue; while purple of amethyst glowed over all. The fins were as tawny as gold river in flood.

This great jewel fish sparkled like ancient king's crown, but then had the face of a deer. Its dark eyes were the color of the boys' very own.

It came from its trap in a splutter and flash, on fins used like legs, smiled kind of a smile, and leapt in a dash. The boys let it go. There was never a question of whether to take as their own. In a blink it was gone. It vanished in the deep with a splash and a sparkle of ruby-red tail. The water around it lit up in a circular wake with a sparkle of garnets and colors of rainbow on grey.

The boys laughed and laughed at a deer-headed fish with the colors and sparkle of great jeweled crown. They bagged up their fish in the large croaker bags that drug heavy on the ground and left trail in the sand. It took half of the day till they got their great bags safely back home, and to Granny's delight. No rabbits to clean; only fish and more fish and some more. What a supper they'd have and a feast and a time!

The men skinned them up with great pliers that shone in the afternoon sun, avoiding the spikes of the whiskers of cat. The great old wash pot was hot from the coals of the cherry, the ash, and the oak. The fish were cut up and simmering long with fresh corn, new potatoes, green onions, herbs, spices, and such—all cooking as one in the single great cast-iron pot.

As the sunset was glowing in first chill of the fall, the feasters drew closer round full pot that bubbled and sang. They came nearer the coals as seated on split-oaken canes of their Granny's own make; they each told their tales of fishing and fish from generations far back, right up to today. From out cauldron of fable the stories rose up like the bubbles of pot that bubbled and sang. Darcy and Nish now took place in the ring with their story of great jeweled fish. There next to their neighbors, four sisters, grownup brother and wife, and their ma and their pa, with their granny and grandpa and newest twin golden nephews beside, the brothers gathered harmonious as one in tight family cirque. Grandpa gave blessing for fish, supper, and day they'd received, for the family and neighbors there gathered, for those gone before and for those yet to come, for the great tawny Tyger who gave them its gift from the grace of the deep, and the bright jeweled Spirit of River, free to frisk, flash, and play.

And no one marveled at today's story of the brothers' great jeweled fish, for the grandpa had caught him the same as his grandsons that day, and at their same age to a dot. No wonder at that! For so had all Grandpa's six sons, and the grandpa's own father and six brothers before. They'd all shared their stories, like now, and, in them, grew one. In shinings and spangles, the great jeweled fish rose out from the soul of the deep to greet each amazed new generation from same cornucopia cone. No one in the family had ever once thought to take the great jeweled Tyger fish home for his own. Instead, it always went free, like the river to flow.

And that is why they'd gather here this night again by ruby-bright coals that lit up their faces in cirque against cold black night at their backs—to eat their great, joyful feast with the living and dead grown harmonious one across time, and perfect as pearl. And that is why they'd sit now as one beneath deep-rooted roof tree and diamond stars, and could trust to the grace of a topaz returning new day.

IX
The Wee One's Alphabet Blocks

Just above the Tyger's wave, on its tree-crested hill, sat the big old house. *Rat-a-tat. Rat-a-tat* came the startling sound once again as regular as clockwork this three A.M. As always, the knocking went on for a time and ended with a great jolting *Slam,* as if a heavy door came shut, or a large weight was dropped on the floor. The sounds always seemed to come from the next story above, whether listener was sleeping on first floor or second. No one at three, startled out of the soundness of sleep, and in the pitch darkness of night, ever found nerve to venture into the pine-floored garret to see if the noise was up there too. *Rat-a-tat. Rat-a-tat. Rat-a-tat.* A loud *Slam.* Then silence again.

It couldn't be the house creaking on its bones, or settling—certainly not after 200 years. What was it then? *Rat-a-tat. Rat-a-tat. Rat-a-tat.* On first floor and second as well.

When we become accustomed to the striking of a clock, we are no longer aware that it strikes loud and long.

At first it keeps us awake, maddens throughout the night; but then it subsides and disappears totally from the front of the brain. So went the nightly performance at three, and the dwellers, grown accustomed, slept soundly on. However, without fail, their guests would tell their stories the next morning in wide-eyed amaze. "What was that *Rat-a-tat,* then *Boom,*" they would half-ask, half-exclaim. No one could answer, and thus the mystery remained to perplex.

Rat-a-tat. Rat-a-tat. Rat-a-tat. As regular as rain on the lead and tin roof, and the mystery remained to perplex.

Then one night a visitor, a poet by trade, slept in the guest room up the great walnut stairs and heard the same startling noise. But for him the *Rat-a-tat* came with a fit-ful strange dream.

Two boys were in this room where he slept. They were well-dressed young lads in neat white linen shirts, silken cravats, and shining black leather shoes. They wore short black pants and square-tailed jackets alike, and had thick thatches of raven-black hair. But for their difference in age, they could have been twins. The elder brother was stu-dious, or trying to be, and sat at the desk of an open secre-tary with gothic arched doors. He was absorbed in a book, as if doing his work for a tutor's assignment or school. He looked the picture of a dignified little gentleman, properly studious and properly behaved, but was no more than ten.

The younger lad was very much still a child, and mis-chievous too. His cravat and collar were loosened, his shirt-tail half out, and he was intent on disturbing the reading above him as he played on the floor. Just learning his *A, B,* and *C*s, he was whiling away this boring time with his alphabet blocks. They were made out of wood and painted in brightest of hues. *Rat-a-tat. Rat-a-tat. Rat-a-tat,* they made sounds as he banged them on shining pine floor.

The great glass panes of the secretary doors reflected his play and displeasure of brother who got increasingly peeved and annoyed. "Stop that, Dickie," he'd say. At which Dickie, as the way of little brothers when challenged and bored, made even louder *Rat-a-tat,* and faster, more insistent *Rat-a-tat—Rat-a-tat—Rat-a-tat* as he banged his blocks on the floor.

The racket increased and its tempo and tempers as well, and finally with great jolting *Slam,* the poet's dream came to an end.

At breakfast, the visitor revealed himself mightily impressed. The vividness of his dream was still present to mind, and it haunted and stayed. The conversation over distraction of big country breakfast of grits, ham, biscuits, fig preserves, scuppernong jelly, coffee, and such kept returning to details of the dream that he finally got down in coherent narrative form. The tale he recounted remained in the back of host's brain, where it eddied and eddied and lodged.

At three of each morn, the noise came faithfully sure. *Rat-a-tat. Rat-a-tat. Rat-a-tat,* and then a great single *Boom.*

The family tree yielded him up names of the lads.

From the cut of their clothes in the dream, they came from midcentury last. And the only two brothers of their age in the Great House at that time were young Dixon and Charles, brothers of dark thatch of hair. Charles was the elder; "Dickie" (as Dixon was called in life and the dream) was the younger of the two. Both brothers had lived all their lives in the house, had been born in its rooms and had died there as well. Dickie lived a full life of great service and use until age ninety-two. By then, his grandchildren were many and made noise of their own. Charles died unmarried at age twenty-four, in this very same room of the dream. He had studied on well, and a good doctor became after three years in medical school. He'd been serious always throughout his short life like the boy in the dream. He died of scarlet fever caught from patients in the year '61. It was epidemic that year in the neighborhood all around, and Charles wore himself down with tending the sick and witnessing loss. When the ravings of his fever settled down, he calmed at the last, and wept that he must leave so many in pain and in need, and his life's work undone.

Our host, who had been drawn deeply now into the magic and mystery of the house, went diligently searching for any facts or a clue as a tie of the place to the past. In a city some miles away, he discovered, descended in Dickie's own family down, the great gothic glass-doored secretary-desk exactly as described in the young poet's dream. It was bought by the brothers' own father and signed in a drawer with his name, and the year 1847.

In another of its drawers was a box with a red-painted wooden toy top and six blocks made out of wood. They were alphabet blocks brightly painted, well worn, and from midcentury last. His jaw dropped in awe.

He then borrowed the blocks in a serious mood and took them straight home to the bedroom upstairs.

There he spent vigil awake until three in the morn with the blocks in his hand. When the *Rat-a-tat* of the ghost blocks began overhead, he nervously accompanied them straight with his own on the floor. *Rat-a-tat* in same rhythm and rhyme. *Rat-a-tat. Rat-a-tat* in the same space in time. *Rat-a-tat. Rat-a-tat. Rat-a-tat,* and then great crashing *Boom.* The quiet returned, somehow deeper than before, a strange stillness and a calm in the room. The blocks, as he'd promised, went back the next day to Dickie's own heirs.

But no more did the sound of the blocks come again in the room. No single time more was the loud *Rat-a-tat* to be heard. No *Rat-a-tat-tat* woke the startled guest from the bed each morning at three. No *Rat-a-tat-tat* was heard on the great walnut stair. No *Rat-a-tat-tat* haunted back of host's brain. But instead, just at four before dawn of each day, a swishing of wings would now wake sleepers from sleep, a flutter of wings like the wind in a whirl brushed their faces in bed, to their startlement and sudden amaze, and their sitting up straight to inquire of the dark. As regular as rain on the lead and tin roof, the wings have come; and the mystery has remained to perplex to this day.

X
Spilt Milk
~ ∾ ~

The shining tin pail struck heavy against the child's bare flank as he walked toward the kitchen. It seemed miles because the pail was so large and the child was so small. The wire handle cut into his palm like the switching he'd get if he spilled. The family needed every drop. Nothing could be wasted or there'd be hungry babes, and with too much spilling, an end to them all. At intervals, he stopped to breathe and change the pail from left to right, from right to left, as he walked.

If he could let his mind wander to happy things, then the wire didn't cut. This he did at present. The foam of the pail's white treasure he saw as pearls, and then the pearls took him to sea, where there were ships with giant white billowing sails he'd heard of but had never seen. His child's imagination was as rich as the cream his mama would skim from the pail, to come out in golden bricks of bright butter, as yellow as doubloons from a pirate's big chest.

In the midst of reverie, his foot struck a root, the pail

spilled, and all but a trace was lost. He sat there and wept till his tears dotted the foam. The thirsty spring earth soaked both up with a zeal, and soon they were gone, leaving no trace as it seemed. "Darden!" he heard his mama call from the house, and her call brought him home. He was late and expected and he came quickly indoors. She needed the milk and to know where he was. Scolded and switched and scolded again, he slipped back to the woods, where hot tears couldn't be seen.

The place where Darden had spilled the milk was a glade just above the pasture and milking sheds. It was dominated by a giant white oak, and it was over one of this tree's roots that his foot had tripped. Here Darden often sat when he was free of chores. He was small, but sure there were many small ways he could help family out, so he was not idle very often and had little time of his own. He stacked wood, carried water and milk, led home the cows, relayed messages to and from the kitchen and fields, toted things back and forth from house to the plow. In summer, he always had care of the water jug for the workers at ends of their rows. When time was short in rush seasons of planting and harvest, he'd carry the dinner pails precisely at noon so the hands would lose no time coming from fields. This he liked to do best. There were laughter and jokes and always the songs of the hands while they worked, and smell of ham biscuits and black-eyed peas and the sweet of the cold, cold tea in great sweating glass mason jars on a hot July day.

But mostly he'd like to go down to the quiet white-oak meadow and sit on a stone. He worked hard as any boy, and took this rare time just to muse. This day of the spilled milk, his flanks still hurt from the bumping of pail overlaid with the switching they'd got. It had been a quick switching with mainly sharp-pointed words, so now his reverie took even the last of the sting away with its balm. His pride was hurt, for he knew he'd failed; but the pearls of foam soon appeared to his mind and found him at sea.

The air was soft as sea-island cotton and the palms swayed back and forth, came and went, mesmerizing like the rise and fall of the white-capped waves. Here there were no cows and kitchens and pails. If you messed up, you got no keen switchings from petticoat rule. You walked the plank in a manly way. You got eaten by fishes, left no trace of your guilt to remain. There was no crying besides. You looked straight at the sea eye to eye and fell in. It was a clean way to end failure, or so the boy concluded in his philosophic stark juvenile way.

But Darden was growing in responsibility with every chore he performed, and he learned best with the occasional spill. Under the gentling branches of oak he was tutored as surely as at fireside of home. Switches, roots, and branches all made up parts of his world. He learned pride in his work and a sense of his duty to the realm lying outside his own smarting skin.

Through the following months, when Darden could forget himself and his work, he would come here to the land spreading out wide under branches of oak. The place where he spilled his pail the very next spring became white with snowdrops, nodding their fragrant white bells, each with the little green dots. And before their appearance, he had sat in the snow on his stone just a few days before. The dun of the oak-leaf-strewn floor, white with last year's spilled milk, had turned white while he slept with the magic of snow, and now again suddenly white with the wavelike nodding of bells.

A wren scolded from the covert of bush. A crow cawed raucously from a distant hill.

Darden himself would turn and transmogrify as rapidly as his magic oak dell, as legs and arms stretched out spindly and long like roots of the tree. He would soon be in what the grown folks called the gangly, the awkward age. He did not quite know what to do with long arms and legs and sometimes tried to hide them, make them seem less obvious to the view. Mostly they seemed just in the way. But the days of switchings had passed, and with them, petticoat rule from kitchen and hearth. Now his father meted out justice stern and severe with words and looks of pleasure for good and displeasure for ill.

As for doing wrong—nothing was now as simple as milk spilled from a pail. There were more roots in the world and his feet seemed to hit them all, as if he were walking in the woods stark blind, strange woods oftentimes with no stars or a moon as a guide.

But some miraculous how, with time, even these

strange paths grew less foreign, more familiar as legs strengthened and lengthened their stride, his feet planted firm. The valley land of his birth echoed loud in his ears when his steps strayed from his home, and soon he returned. Without knowing they would, his legs always found certain sure way to the giant old oak and his stone, like a compass, always pointing him true. Seated under its branches, the white of spilled milk now turned to white of his head; and his head nodded silent in drowse of a hot August noon, like the nodding of magic and familiar white bells in his boyhood's own spring.

XI

How Jakob Emig Encountered Old Scratch

From the front porch, Jakob Emig could look across fields where his winter wheat greened nicely. An old man now, with his sons gone off to war, he lived mainly in a woman's world of married daughters and daughters-in-law on farms scattered nearby. He lived alone, widowed now for two years, hard work during wartime finally having taken its toll on his wife's constitution already weakened by a series of illnesses. She'd borne him seven living children, and he was remembering her now on the front gallery as Old Zeke lay at his feet, nose outstretched on paws and wrinkling eyes upward to his master. There would be no hunting today, though the hound eagerly waited for any sign of preparation.

Jakob was remembering back nearly forty years ago when he and his Polly first began farming these fields and built this house. It had started log-modest and been added to and clapboarded over the years. The old one-room cabin with fireplace large enough to stand in had eventually become the kitchen onto which he built a big four-room house. When the girls came along, he'd also made shed-room additions.

He and Polly had lost four babes to sudden fevers and unexplained illnesses. The Lord's will. They buried them in the hillside plot and grieved. It was to these lost little ones and to Polly, fresh and young in her homespun linen, that his mind returned mostly, to Polly and himself in the wagon going to church the first Sunday after their marriage, sitting together that day in the little sanctuary where men and women always sat apart for worship. Newlyweds had this privilege for a time, and he remembered how the congregation wished them well, out of full hearts. These were his neighbors whom he thought of now in turn. Some who had died—how the years had treated others—how they were bearing up in these evil and trying times. Remembering then the firstborn, taken from them with fever that first spring, and how Polly took it so hard it was like to kill her too, and he so low that the planting dragged on forever. But they had had to put it aside and carry on, for they were strong folk and meant to make a go. Their people before them had done the same on the same land under hardships far worse than these. Too, Providence had given them special powers and strengths that would always prevail against the forces of evil.

It was in the middle of these thoughts that he saw the first column of smoke. It rose slowly and distinctly like a dark stain on a linen-white sky. Although it was far enough distant, he knew that he must soon rise now and see to the livestock. He would need to hide it as best he could in the surrounding deep woods. He must also see to putting the meal and hams in sacks for burial. When the second and third columns rose to right and left of the first, he knew he must be stirring. Old Zeke whimpered. There was something in his master's movements that made him anxious. Jakob's mind was far from the hunt, and he rose stiffly from the split-bottomed chair to go first to smokehouse, then to kitchen. He worked with method, efficiently and deftly, but without hurry, tying the cords stiffly with old man's hands. The hams went into canvas bags that he had made several days ago for the purpose.

He had already dug his holes the week before on the dry slope of a hill in the proper thickets where they could be covered with leaves and brush. It was a matter of only a few hours until he had hitched Towse to the wagon and, Zeke at his heels, had buried four fine hams, three canvas-covered barrels of meal, and one of flour.

This would see him through the rest of winter, and his boys and daughters as well. The boys, God willing, would return one day soon; their farms were not faring as well as his own, having no grown menfolk to take proper reins. The gals were strong and plowed well enough; but there was too much to be done, and the oldest grandson on any of the farms was ten. Yes, there would be hungrier mouths to feed than now, and a long time till harvest. God only knew what these next six months would have in store for them. Jakob could only trust and do all in his power.

His feet made icy prints as he went about his early

work. There had been a heavy frost this February morning, and by eleven it was still unmelted. The white sun's rays seemed to have no force in them; he could not feel them on his shoulders. The columns of dark smoke now rose everywhere in the pale sky. They were close. The one to the immediate left was, he knew, in the direction of his eldest son John's, some three miles distant. He raised a prayer for Christiana as he bridled his mules and led them from the lot. He just could not be with them all, and prayed God to hold them in His hands. He had wanted to call them all together under his protecting wings but knew they were too independent and practical for that, wishing to care for the homesteads that their husbands had left them in trust. Old Zeke, the two milk cows, the three sheep, the yoke of oxen, and the two beeves, he tethered and hid as best he could away from the sight of the house in the distant woods. He muttered a few words in a foreign tongue over them. As this was accomplished and he was returning home, he saw the smoke from his barn and caught a glimpse of blue men on horseback switching and swirling in his yard. It was time for him to think about himself and his own safety.

Smoke seemed to ring him. Somewhere to the distant east, the woods had caught fire. The sky was raining soot and cinders and was pitch black. The world itself seemed to be on fire, and the white sun seldom shone through the breaks of smoke. Jakob could now hear the intermittent pop and crackle of occasional musketry, and the laughs and shouts of bearded mouths. Somebody seemed to be having lots of fun; he knew it wasn't him. He would have to exercise all his strength to keep himself from defending his farmstead with the rifle that rested impotently over his mantel. Common sense and the ring of smoke taught him that such an attempt would be of no gain. He was one against thousands, and an old man besides.

Yet he had little fear for his own safety, for he had tricks up his threadbare sleeves that even Satan-helped Northmen wouldn't believe. Theirs were the powers of darkness and a cinder-dark sky over which light would prevail. Their element was Satan's dark fire and they brought death, ashes, and destruction in the paths that they trod. He himself exercised powers as ancient as theirs and more fearful by a long shot. He needed neither torch nor rifle. Time would just have to tell who would come out better here.

Jakob had that reputation. Both he and Polly practiced what the good farm folk of the area called *using,* or *Brauchen,* in the old German tongue of their ancestors. He was known far and wide for his wizardry, in a community in which *users* were numerous and properly respected. Folks even came from far off to seek his help. Among *users,* he truly had no equal. All acknowledged it, and he knew it. Were it not for his gentle nature and trustworthiness, he would have been universally feared, and properly so. His own recognition of his powers, however, went almost as far as pride, which Jakob was always heedful of having to guard against. It was his one real weakness, and he knew that too. Just where these mysterious powers came from, he himself did not comprehend. He only knew he had them; and because they were special gifts, he had learned early that he must take care to practice them humbly, sparingly, and only for the good. That they must be practiced so must have been a requirement for their potency, for the one time that he sought to do otherwise, he failed and failed miserably, to his own considerable physical discomfort.

This time, and in these circumstances, he knew he'd not fail. The fires of hell were flaming around him, and Satan's emissaries were brandishing torch and terrible swift swords. He eased a bit closer to see their devilish work, to the orchard within a hundred paces of his burning barn. Near him the blue men were having carnival in the glare of the fire, emptying his smokehouse. One soldier was stringing ropes of sausages around his neck like a necklace of pearls. Another wore a dead chicken on his head like a great feather bonnet. A trickle of its crimson blood ran in a thin line into the soldier's hair and down onto his neck. What they could not carry off, they were intent on destroying. Jakob looked on sadly, and his only solace was that Polly was not there to see what was happening to the fruits of many hard years of work, careful planning, struggle, and sacrifice—all gone in a matter of hours. But Jakob was sure he would yet have the last word, and properly so. He knew his strength, if only he managed to practice it humbly, with fitting restraint, and without anger or malicious intent.

Before he could put his plan in motion, however, he

felt a cold barrel pressed to the small of his back and heard the sinister click of a hammer readying for fire. He had been captured by the Northmen, sure as sin, and was being marched into his own yard as a prisoner. Where was his gold? He had no gold. Where was his silver? He had no silver. Where were his shiny jewels and valuables? He had none. "We will just see about that for ourselves," they assured, "and if you are lying, you will surely die."

His house was already being ransacked from garret to cellar. He saw his old faithful rifle being carried away. Polly's quilts were being strung on horses for saddle blankets and the rest were being torn, sabred, and trampled. Every chest had been brought into the yard and knocked apart. The other furniture was likewise brought outside and made the targets for both rifle and sword, then smashed and ridden over by the horses. He looked on with amazement and sullen disbelief. The whole scene had the quality of dream.

They had not found gold, they said. Where was it? They would shoot him if he did not tell them where he had hidden it. They knew he lied, they said; but he did not. Soon, soon, now, he would have to use his power against them. If only he could remain cautious and humble so as not to anger the Almighty.

They took him to his barnyard, in the glare of his burning barn, and into his poultry lot. Here, every creature had been decapitated and those not taken away for camp dinner were still strewn about in twitching and headless state. His old peacock, his wife's fondest pet, lay shot through the head near its favorite perch at the gate. A sad sight, but he had always been a proud strutter and a vain gazer into pools at himself. A soldier had been annoyed by his pride and his sudden loud cry as if mocking the Great Army in Blue.

Jakob looked on patiently. No, he did not lie about the gold; so they placed him with his back against the poultry house and began to shoot musket balls about his head to force him to tell them where it was. A Minié ball came close to his left ear. Its sound was like the buzz of a big green horsefly or an enormous mosquito. Splinters from the fractured wood behind him grazed his cheek and drew a small trickle of red. He could not tell them where nonexistent gold was hidden, so they were about to kill him. For his own self, it did not matter overmuch. He was old and had had a good life and would just as lief be with Polly again; but there were his children and grandchildren, who would need his help in the lean raven days ahead. He could give them his hams and help them get going again. For he knew that at this very same moment their farms were being laid waste in the same way as his own, as truly they were. The ring of fire around him was from the lands of his children and closest of kin.

The right ear now, pop and buzz, and the next ball would likely take his life. As he watched the blue man with the red beard pull trigger and the rifle flash its long orange streak, he lined the ball as it issued from the barrel, as it

aimed and sped for his forehead, slowed it, struggled with
it to twist it out of its path so that when it resumed its
velocity, it went flying at a forty-five-degree angle into a
great black iron wash pot. There it spun round and round,
making a tinny sound, till it stopped silent. The blue men
were amazed. One walked to the pot and picked up the bullet. Jakob stood calm. He served the second, third, fourth,
and fifth bullets in the very same way. Each time the ball
went *Phling* into the giant wash pot. Several different men
tried with different muskets, but each time, the bullets
went *Phling* into the giant wash pot. By now, there were
many blue men gathered. The thirteenth bullet clanged and
spun *Phling* into the pot and was retrieved in the shape of a
tiny lead cross. This ended the experiment at once. Most of
the men, though they tried to bluster it off, began to fear.
However, the first soldier, the loud and red-bearded man
who had been drinking, was angered rather than frightened.

He fumbled at his left side and fixed his bayonet, then
made to lunge at the old man. As Jakob lined the bayonet
that was aimed at his heart, he fought with it with his eyes
and froze its motion within a foot of him. The red-bearded
soldier writhed and twisted behind the bayonet frozen in
midair, trying to move it, then tried to free himself from it,
but found that his skin was stuck, as if to ice. He thrashed
about in all manner of grotesque motions, comic to behold
if they had not been so desperately performed. It was at this
moment that he of the red beard looked Jakob in his steely-
grey eyes. Jakob's eyes calmed him, transfixed him as on

the point of a bayonet, and froze him in midstruggle. There stood Red Beard, with glazed eyes fixed on Jakob, one foot lifted from the ground in the motion of plunging forward, his hands frozen to the instrument. To Jakob, he looked for the world like Old Zeke on his most famous point when a larger-than-usual covey of bobwhites would fly into view.

It was then that the other blue men began to fear in earnest. A few had heard that such wizards existed in this strange backwater land through which they passed. In their march of burning, they had just yesterday seen three tall, gaunt sisters dressed in flowing black garments come onto the porch of an old farmhouse nearby, chanting and wailing in an unknown tongue. These weird sisters had caused shivers, surrounded as they were with a surreal landscape of desolate burned stumps, ashes, and fire, and the blue men passed them in quiet, sparing their house from the usual pillage and burning out of an unreasoned fear. What, then, were they encountering here? Was it more of the same wizardry and craft? Thoughts of gold and silver vanished from minds obsessed with its gain.

Meanwhile, Jakob stood silent and calm in the strength of his powers. He no longer spoke. He was no longer spoken to. As he moved for the first time, taking a step to the side of the frozen bayonet aimed at his chest, the semicircle of blue men shrank back from him. They opened outward to let his gaunt form pass. Jakob then walked the short distance to his house, gazed at by all, but molested by none.

The home, now having been completely plundered of booty, was about to be burned. As Jakob approached, a Black Beard on a roan horse accosted him with lightning-swift sword. Jakob fought with his eyes and froze both man and beast, the man with sword uplifted and dark eyes glazed. The same he did with two threatening men on foot, struggling with their eyes and freezing them in midstride.

There was another Red Beard with torch in hand about to fire the dimity curtains of the front parlor window. He looked at Jakob as he was about to apply the torch and caught his calm steely-grey eyes. Jakob struggled with Red Beard's frantic eyes, in which the fires from the torch reflected, and froze the man in calmness. The torch fire melted into water, which froze as a long icicle that dripped from the soldier's outstretched hand. The figure, it would look for the world like the statue of the cold iron-green woman, torch in her hand, to be built decades hence in the great smoky harbor of the Northmen's own home.

These scenes were witnessed by more than a few, who now shrank back from our wizard, who calmly went about his business. The woods had caught fire from the burning barn and smokehouse. These threatened with their sparks the very farmhouse itself.

Thus Jakob, now given wide berth, especially since the presence of the five frozen statue-men attested quite graphically and persuasively to his powers, was able to move undisturbed. He slowly circled his and Polly's dwelling— once, twice, three times while *using* with the incantation long taught by his own. The blue men watched in awe and astonishment akin to horror as Jakob went about his solemn ritual. The three weird sisters of yesterday could not hold a candle to this, though the pair of events had the result of reinforcing one another in potency of effect in the aliens' brains. Like most bullies, these men were cowards and could swagger around women, old men, and children, but with danger to themselves now a possibility for the first time, they hastened away, some leaving chickens roasting on spits, some in the middle of looting the springhouse, fleeing with moustaches of cream still on their lips.

The booty wagons on which the goods from his house had been piled now hastened to pull out. With a glance of his eye, Jakob locked their wheels, as if an iron bar had been thrust into them. The men on them fell forward with a jolt, quickly dismounted, cut loose their horses, and fled in a rout. The wagons sat quiet in the lane with a golden sheen of enchantment spread over them like one of Polly's best yellow-tulip quilts.

Jakob was soon again alone with five statues, but not for long. As was usually the case during the great march of destruction, the conquerors came in waves. It was not long until another, bigger band of blue soldiers, this time headed by Gen. Judson Kilpatrick himself, rode into Jakob's yard.

Jakob had charmed the fire so that it burned to the magic circle, and it did not cross this line. The charred and smoking weeds ran up to the unburned grass to form a perfect ring. Further, no man but Jakob was able to enter it.

His house was thus saved; his livestock and goods were secure in the charmed woods, where no foot could touch down, and frankly he was a bit weary from all the commotion. Too, *using* exhausts a body so. And this new red-bearded one on the great black horse Jakob correctly knew to be Satan himself; the smell of Lucifer matches and burning sulfur was about him; and Jakob had sense enough to know that even *using* powers had their limits. His eyes could not struggle with Satan's to extinguish their myriad dark fires, and one could not look into the doors to Red Beard's burning abyss without being affected somehow for the worse, contaminated in some sort of central way of spoiling and wounding. The Scriptures always had taught him to leave evil alone, to give it respectful safe distance alway. So Jakob thus rightly felt it best to avoid this man named Kilpatrick and his blood-red-bearded twin brother, Sherman, himself seen in the wizard's inner eye as he skulked somewhere across the river in the nearby shadowed woods of burning Fairfield. Kilpatrick and his men could do no more damage to him after all, and Jakob must be careful not to overstep the bounds into pride in his powers. So he, with a wink of his left steely-grey eye, the one with the yellow flecks in it, turned himself into a great log by the garden palings. Here he could witness the conclusion of the little drama in which he had up to now been the central actor.

There, as a solid pine log, he was feeling comfortable, smug, and superior. You might say he was even coming close to a damaging pride. So to chasten him, the Almighty (felt Jakob) brought him appropriately low by having Judson Kilpatrick sit on him to eat his midday meal while he puzzled over the deserted, frozen, and well-filled booty wagons and the five statues that used to be men.

Long years since, Jakob, now grown to a truly venerable age and an honored patriarch in the land, would tell us from his spot in the chimney corner the tale of this day. To the thrilled and hushed amazement of his legion of great-grandchildren, he would recall that of all the losses he'd suffered, and of all the troubles and trials of the day, the one thing that stung him most was having Satan's backside imprinted upon him. The Almighty caused it to happen, however (he was quick to tell us children), out of an infinite wisdom not to be questioned. Jakob had saved his hearth and home, but Satan had shown an awesome power before which he could nevermore be too vain. These were truly all lessons worth the learning, and of how to use power aright—even if he'd had to be pressed by Satan's own backside to know.

And his last greatest magic of all: "I'll be talking after I'm dead," we'd once heard him say. And sure he still is, for his stories live on, and so do his truths.

XII
The Magnolia Fay

~ ⟨∞⟩ ~

It is deep in the opening bell that I dwell—deep, deeper than noon of a lemon-pale light, to sit in the cool summer dusk in the middle of luminous bloom around clustering fingers of cone. My seat at the center is regal enough for a canopied throne. I curl in, and around, and then rise from my drowse, to dance with bare toes on the tapestried tip of the cone. I play my tattoos all around in arabesque design. My limbs are the color of pale lemon light, like the color of honeycomb cone. They are long and supine, and made for the dance. My hair is the burnt sunset red of cone's base and the tips of its fingers that lie in a whorl.

The wings of the blossoms open white all around, shining white as sea-pearls and foam from the wave. It is then that I wake most fully from out a deep dream. I dance in the wind of a soft Southern twilight on petals that glow like my skin, on petals as living and smooth as my skin. New light from the moon will call me out wholly in air. The air it is heavy with smell of the bloom, none other alike—heavy dripping with honey and nectared ambrosia, thick richest perfume of the woods and the earth. It is caught in the folds of my swirling and fiery red hair that tangles and flies like the rays from the late purpling sun.

The flower's shining great petals are my stage as I twirl. The cone is my center and I dance in a whirl. I circle and weave in quite dizzy a spell, and grow dizzy myself from the circling dance and the thick, heavy smell. The song that I sing is the song of the whirring great luna moth and long-legged firefly. It has never beginning, nor ever a close.

Fireflies are friends and my subjects, and all serve me well. They work busily round and feed on the nectar that I set in gold lotus-shaped bowls. I ride them like steeds abroad in the night; and they neigh and gallop and speed. They light up the dark with their lamps like the great glowing blossom I bear, themselves making flowers in air that fly and dart and flicker and flee. They rest and are fed in their stalls in the stable of bloom, the heart of my heart.

Out comes the moon, and we two are to reign now supreme, the queen of the night with the queen of the vanishing brief beauty of earth. Moon's light against leaves that are deeper than onyx or jade cannot be resisted; and out from the houses of men, daughters and sons issue forth for a stroll. I play hide-and-seek on the lip of each dimple of petal of pearl, and hop-skip-and-jump from each dimple to dimple around. Some see me, some not; for some I am shy, and for some I am not.

The moon rides up high and I am aware of its place. I

lean and I yearn to it always in wide arc around. My dance is toward it, as it is my audience fair. It applauds with its light, gives bravos and flowers and praises and blossoms some more.

The flower full open, its shining wings out and full flared, I walk stately forth, with my own wings outspread as mirror to shine. Moon smiles in its beams of approval for dancer and actress, performance so rare. I bow and I bow and my red hair falls down from my ruby- and emerald- and pearl-crusted crown. I make exit to rest and to sleep. Dawn approaches, rose-pink morn breaking soon, and moon-dials are set for the sleep of the day. I curl around base of the deep, deep fragrance of flower till my toes touch my crown and I drowse and I dream. Full circle I am, like the flower itself, and the whirlwind that bore me, and the earth and the moon. Begin not, nor end, I exist as I am.

My petals, my luminous wings, they grow tattered ecru, wan yellowed lace, then turn brown. They droop and they fall to the ground, and my throne rises up now to wax and to grow and turn purple with seed for the child that will follow the fay, and live long, and then longer than long.

I hum circling my song, in my sleep, no beginning, no end. At the dusk by the chime of moon-dials, you may seek me again in the deep, deep drowse of the cone, spreading my luminous wings to the moon like new moth from the chrysalis born, for the dance that is neither then new, nor yet old, begins not, nor ends, with the great fragrant Laurel in bloom.

XIII

The Revenge of the Great House

To kill a house where great men grew up, married,
died, I here declare a capital offence.
— William Butler Yeats, *Purgatory*

Very much the city man in L. L. Bean shirt and Eddie Bauer pants, he came cross the river quoting Thoreau. In his polished leather valise, he had stored and brought who knows what. As nervous as a black cat crossing an interstate, he was eager to get inside, out of the woods and off the soil. He insistently did not want to see the beans and okra in his host's fields, of which his host was justifiably proud. Books were his game and he had an assignment, a mission to be on. Roughing it, to him, meant no AC.

The subject of the book from his Great Northern Publishing House was the host's own old farm and farmhouse, a very fine Southern plantation, in fact, in its day. His concern was a chapter that dealt with the tenants and slaves who a century and a half ago had lived on this land— one chapter in twenty, but enough to set scurrying Great Publisher's historian advisors, outside readers, inside readers, marketers, copyeditors, managing editors, acquisition editors, editor in chief, and all. What would the world think? In this chapter were no whips, no manacles, no chains, no sighing over proletariats oppressed. "But the records don't show any whips or chains," the author meekly explained. The visitor wanted the chapter changed nevertheless (perhaps a few lashes? a manacle or two? perhaps a few chains?) to satisfy markets and to garner reviews in (hold your breath) the great *New York Times Book Review.* All in the office had read and reread for two weeks and concurred. The historian advisor who came with him expressed himself officially "quite agreed."

The author of the book in question, who lived in this place, and knew it at night, kept his peace. He'd encountered the same sort of talk elsewhere, but had been led to think different of Great Northern Publishing House when the contract for the book had been signed. The praise from the editors flowed like champagne at a big penthouse party on the fiftieth floor of a high-rise in large City-on-Hill, and no mention at all of rewriting a word. The editor's emphasis then had fallen on big sales, big printings, royalties, awards, film scripts, and such.

So it was quite a surprise when our city Thoreau came on mission with leather valise.

The author (we'll just call him Bob) was expecting a nice social call, maybe a walk to the river, some putting up feet on porch bannisters, leisurely passing the time of a hot summer day, allowing his visitors to learn the slow rhythms of place and seeing firsthand the subject of book they were set to bring out to the world. But he should have suspected that Henry Davids all come to such places as his (without AC) only to get books for Cities-on-Hills (with AC), where people could read of sweat in hot summer fields under vents of AC. Then with mission accomplished, Editor Thoreau would quickly move on, book in one hand in the form that would sell, and a contract in the other, declaring how the paths of one culture were getting too worn to the pond, so his adventuresome, expansive, great-hearted spirit would lead him to new shining Waldens and different bright morning stars. (The stars were the size and the shape of great shiny dollars more often than not.) The hypocrisy of this was not lost on our Bob, who had lived with it often enough among alien elite.

No, our Editor (we will call him Henry after his god) was not aware that Thoreau from his Walden took his clothes home to mama every weekend to clean, or that just over the trees, Concord church bells rang loud at his cabin on pond. Or that an easy short walk brought him to Waldo Emerson's comfy house on the prim village green for confab and a crumpet and tea, which Waldo would have sent up to his mouth in helicopters where his head lived in the fog and muddle of clouds. No, our Henry was not aware that Thoreau was a hater of all human flesh but his own, and dealt comfortably only with abstracts in his cold city man's way. No community for him, no ties to a past—as cold and bland as a codfish and as solitary too.

Our Henry would not stay to share meal with their host. This he stated abruptly and as sharply as razor cuts meat, and he charged for the shiny new car, historian in tow. Henry unlocked his Land Rover from a distance with a mechanized toy, and stroked its sparkling new paint upon entering, all while quoting Thoreau. Then they were off—that is, ten yards toward the gate. The Land Rover spluttered and wheezed, then sank in on its sports-vehicle's fashionable self. It had died in the yard, and for all its great cost the engine would not hit a lick. Not the battery sure, tank full of gas, lines full of oil. Must be malfunction in fail-proof and fool-proof car computer that controlled all in all.

So Henry got out, with historian at heel. He gave orders to Gibbon, "Call Triple A!" and off Gibbon went as his master had bid, while the sound of command rumbled down all the hills like the thunder of Zeus. Yes, indeed, "Call Triple A!" That's all they could do. Out here in the woods, no garage in the country was near, nor a store. Not a taxi, a bus, rent-a-car, or a train.

Shadows lengthened on lawn. The evening grew dusk into dark, and Thoreau had found him a thick book to read, as thick as his head. He came armed with a spare everywhere that he went just in case of emergencies like these. On either airline or train, he could hide behind book and not have to converse and engage. His historian opted to snore on the sofa with head in the crook of his arm. Bob wondered at all that transpired on this day, and labored to take all in stride.

The home where he lived, he loved for its beauty and

calm, its links to his people and culture's own past—to the brave men and women who kept it and loved it for their own little time. Its lifeblood was farming and good rich land, not machines of the asphalted Cities-on-Hills. He loved deeply the gentle folds of blue hills that surrounded his home, the deep flowing river below, the crops and the pastures, the furrows he tilled. He loved deer and the turkey, the redbird and quail, the swallow, the red-tail, the phoebe and wren, even foxes and 'possums, and creatures that crawled. It was the place of his birth and of fathers and mothers before. To make it a harsh world of hate in a class-struggle way would be alien to place. He lived in his subject, and would never betray with a lie, no matter the riches, acclaim, or the prize.

For besides being a real place that he touched with his hands, it was Coole Park and Penshurst, Appleton House, Chatsworth, Pemberley. As Fair Saxham to Thomas Carew. Only difference, he lived in his subject and no visitor he, on a tour or a whim. But he shared with these august great writers of old the very same love. Harmonious style, high aspirations, the good life sheltered within, in countryside fertile, in tune with the seasons of year, in harmony with men. Now in valise of a city Thoreau, passing through, it would be classic Class Struggle, one more burnt offering to *Egalité.*

Our host also loved the old place for his family's sake, as the seat of his lineage and line. It was familiar and personal, not just an abstraction in the way of Thoreaus. Yes, he knew the place well, in its moods, sun and shade, day and night, and a lifetime on soil. To betray was to violate heart of himself. This war waged on the culture of what its noble Great Houses meant, he could not understand. It came of self-hate and was suicidal in the extreme. At best, it was absurd; at worst demonic, chaotic in rage. And those who waged it were gloomy and colder than ice. Yes, they hated themselves and practiced self-murder each day. The spawn of the Puritan in their Mather-created Cities-on-Hills had always despised their own nature as men and hated all others for not hating themselves. They hated not only the dance and the song and the wild, but also their flesh and their blood, and embraced instead of all these, abstract and vague new secular gods. Yes, this was the alien culture of death that spawned our Thoreau, and a foreign tradition flawed right from the start. Now it was dragging the world to destruction in its own wicked wake. As for our host, he would refuse to be party to murder of self, for on that very topic his trusty King James was sure and had final, absolute say. Where God puts a period, you never replace with a comma or big question mark. Bob would try to stay clear of this culture of death.

So ran the host's thoughts as Thoreau read his book and Gibbon loud snored.

Bob was late with his chores, but he did them by dark, and he brought in the okra, tomatoes, and all. Figs weighted the trees, and apples depended at door. The scuppernongs hung heavy with bronze clusters on the arbor a few steps away. Late plums fell, feeding the deer. These must wait till tomorrow; he now had no time to do more.

No Triple A in sight, Thoreau wondered what was happening at his office, missed the clutter of his desk and the comfort of his chair. He tried to call in, but it was too late. The staff had left to get ahead of the traffic and scurried down their car-choked lanes to their air-conditioned cells in their suburban house clones, to be selfish together each to each, and there, in the shadow of City-on-Hill, eat up countryside complete.

Thoreau went back to his book. Here, in this old plantation house, he was reading Harriet Beecher Stowe. His valise had his vitamins, health foods, antacids, Valium, and pills; and so he'd not take a supper gathered fresh from the fields by his host, who was no longer surprised. The historian still snored, with dreams of awards, promotions, book reviews, the future, utopia, and such. These, like visions of sugar-plums, danced in his head, and jostled each other in the wide, empty space of his brain, a big abstracted dancerless ballroom, bare with all furniture removed.

Truly, this had been a very bad day for Thoreau. First thing, he'd packed the wrong map in his valise, but then got him a new one at a convenience store, and found the right exit on the Great Interstate. But then on the country roads leading to the house, he got lost three times, made three wrong turns, because, as he said, all plowed fields and farms look the same. The historian was in charge of the turns, and made all the wrong ones each time it could be done.

Put out from the start, Thoreau was now fit to be tied. His new sports vehicle was shot, and he'd have to spend the night in the woods without his AC. Where *was* Triple A? He did all that he could to calm down his nerves—not by looking at the place, taking walks in the wood, or strolling the grounds, not by talking to host (who had stories to tell), or eating fish from the river, fresh food from the fields—no, instead by reading a book. *Uncle Tom* was better (almost) than his portable drugstore of pills.

Bedtime drew on, and still no Triple A. They must have made the same wrong turns by anonymous farms. The host yawned, for soon there'd be another day, and chores to perform, work to do, and a life to be led. But Thoreau, more anxious than ever, read his Stowe with even greater intent, and Gibbon still snored, missing it all.

The old house creaked on its bones, itself yawned like the host in the cool, but as if just waking up, not emptying and readying for sleep. The lightning bugs were out and signaling mates with their lamps; the magnolias yielded their fragrance through the great open doors and tall windows both upstairs and down. It was deep night and past time for all in the house, but the Great House itself, to be dead asleep.

Thoreau was shown upstairs to his four-poster bed. The historian was left on the sofa to snore on his own. No need to wake him to send him to sleep.

The host slept downstairs in his and his wife's cozy bedroom by the great fireplace wall. She was visiting her mother, so he too was alone in a masculine world.

All fell quiet except for the historian's snores, and Bob, tired out from work of the day, fell quickly to untroubled sleep. The Great House's eyes, however, were now open wide, and acutely aware of a presence that must be expelled. Sought and found in the great poster bed was Thoreau, the alien, like sharp-pointed pebble in toe of a shoe, briar point broken off in crook of the finger or crease of the hand, sand grit in the eye, or tick on the dog. It must be removed.

So at three in the morn, the shrill cry of a child woke Thoreau from already dream-tortured sleep of account books unbalanced, bad New York reviews, stock shares in decline. He sat bolt upright to stare at a skull on his chest. The moon was a full one, and its beams spotlighted bone in a phosphorous glow. The child chaunted an agonized song of decapitated cultures slain in their beds and who must have their revenge. As for the agents of genocide, they must stare at slain head straight in the dark hollow sockets of eyes till their own sockets would be robbed of the use of their orbs. The books that these agents had published in reaching their goal would be stacked high on their chests until breath came no more. Was it real or a dream?

For this once, our Thoreau did not pause to riddle it well, the abstract *ins* and *outs* of the choice—the calculated assets and perks (not to mention comforts and dollars) to be gained from the choice of a yes or a no. As always, the choice for such careerists as he would be calculated for sole profit to self, no matter the pious excuses to make those on the take, those on the make, feel good at the same time they are helping themselves from the till, profiting by picking the bones of a culture they'd slain.

This time, none of this, and no time. He jumped from the bed with a scream, and losing his balance and dashing his frame into the great library shelves, he caught hold of a corner in effort to keep from going flat down. In this effort, he pulled the whole wall of books, crashing on him from head to his toe. There were thirteen shelves of walnut and oak from baseboard to crown in this high-ceilinged, high-manteled room. The shelves were all crammed with a family's collection of books beloved, two centuries worth.

There were four oversized volumes of Palladio's works on the architecture of Great Houses, Dante's *Commedia* (in heavy hand-tooled leather), Shakespeare's big first folio, a five-pound folio of Virgil's *Georgics* and *Eclogues,* an over-sized illustrated Horace, a hefty complete Sir Philip Sidney, a weighty complete Spenser, and Malory's *Morte D'Arthur.*

There were Blake's Trianon folios, and Audubon's Elephant Folio of American Birds. There were a great Gutenberg facsimile bigger than the first, several oversized King Jameses, a mammoth Dean Swift, the whole works of King Alfred the Great, Lawrence's *Seven Pillars of Wisdom* (and his *Crusader Castles* as well, itself as heavy as a castle's hearthstone), editions complete of Theocritus, Chesterton, Belloc and Evelyn Waugh, Austen and Eliot, Thackeray, Dickens and Pound, Walker Percy and Faulkner, T. H. White and Ford Madox Ford.

There were eighteenth-century translations of Homer that weighed near fifteen stone, great heavy botanical books, and an illustrated complete Yeats—poems, plays, and prose. His Coole Park poems were each specially mounted on the shelves in heavy gilt frames.

There were Hardy, Cervantes, and Fielding that fell heavy like lead, and Catherine the Great speaking weightily on that bloody French head-chopping monster *Egalité.* There were English Distributists, *I'll Take My Stand,* Lytle and Davidson, complete Wendell Berry and more—and the *pièce de résistance,* entire unabridged Gilmore Simms in every edition he published in life and that weighed nearly a ton.

These made quite a racket as they fell on Thoreau, bringing him flat down to earth (for once) in his fall. A whimper he made like the self-indulged child that he was, from out of the pile that covered him quite. Under the sheer weight of a culture maligned but that lived on in words, he died with "To Penshurst" stuck to one open eye, and *The Waste Land* crammed full in his mouth. The thundering curse of the poet could distinctly be heard in the sound of the crash echoing from out Great House's walls.

Bob sat up at once, saying, "Damn! What the hell!" Then silence again, while the historian turned his head on the sofa and continued to snore. When Gibbon awoke to results of the night, his feelings about his host's own book had miraculously changed, and quickly at that!—you might say, overnight. The book stayed as written; Great Publishing House changed not a word. Gibbon, who fled on foot down the long twisty road, neither returned to the house, nor advised on more books. With Editor gone, Great Publishing House soon folded its Bedouin tent a scant few years thence, and did no more great cultural ill. The culture of death had claimed one of its satisfied own. Thus ended for the time the Great House's curse and revenge.

That same night of the books' great crashing fall, it is said that the sídhe came in a whirling, bright, ilex-leaved wind and, dressed in best jackets of green, wove garlands of foxglove and cowslip over the seven lone steps of the Great House at Coole. They danced in her ruined stone walls in the great whirling wind. The morning thereafter, the sun gleamed gold in the bright thousand panes of Penshurst and Longleat, like great flaming gems, as the grounds of Fair Saxham and Pemberley greened and their long galleries of pictures shone in the burnishing dawn. But most ghostly, that night before dawn, at Thoor Ballylee, the heavy stone staircase anchored deep in the soil gyred up to explode its steps into stars from the ramparts of home, and the bones of all Great Houses, long fallen before, stirred in their graves, then yawned as they breathed them awake.

XIV
Dolphus and the Balking Mule

Now Dolphus was an humble man, but a man of many skills. He could line a bee to a honey tree in the woods pretty near as fast and busy as the bee itself. He could hit on an old plow point and call down a swarm of wild bees right out of the sky. He could smoke and rob a hive with no gear on, and get no sting a-tall. All of us in the neighborhood knew it; he was good with bees, and that wasn't all.

He always puffed away on a great reed-stemmed pipe with a bright-red clay bowl. He used War-Horse tobacco and carried it everywhere with him in its white cotton drawstring pouch. The smoke from his pipe always announced him, and so did his rollicking song.

Yes, Dolphus was an humble man, and a man of many skills, but a man particular in his way. One day he was out removing the combs from fifteen hives for a great squire of the land. Dolphus, as all of us knew, was the best at it, so the Squire, always used to the best, called him in. The Squire, whose name was Didapper, had a fine Great House,

101

broad gardens and orchards and vineyards and pastures and fields, and servants to tend them a-plenty. The smoke from Dolphus's pipe was so delicious that the old Squire hankered after a puff. Dolphus, between puffs on his pipe that sent smoke billowing up in a cloud round his head, was singing "Boil Them Cabbage Down," and had just gotten to the stanza

> *'Possum up a 'simmon tree.*
> *Raccoon on the ground.*
> *Raccoon said to 'Possum, "Sir,*
> *Shake some 'simmons down."*

when Squire Didapper said to Dolph: "Now, Dolph, your pipe smells so good, I must have me a puff." To which Dolph replied, "Why shore. And certainly a puff ye shall have."

Dolphus handed his old reed-and-clay straightway to the Squire. But Didapper, for all his eagerness, did not straightway puff away as Dolph expected he would. Instead, Didapper, who was all gussied up just fit to kill, took a fine linen handkerchief from out of his silk vest just by his heavy gold watch chain, and shook it out with great authority and air of command, displaying his blue monogrammed initials in all corners four. With this, he wiped and scrubbed at the stem. Wiped and scrubbed. Scrubbed and wiped. Wiped and scrubbed some more until he was satisfied it was clean. Dolphus watched as old Didapper then puffed to solid content, then gave back the stem.

Now, Dolphus, as we've said, was an humble man, and

a man of many skills, but a man particular in his way. He was a fellow who didn't mind opening a can of whoop-ass on ary a man who riled him. Several months later, Squire Didapper called on him again. This time it was over a recalcitrant mule. Old Redbone, in the midst of plowing a row, would just stick up his mule ears straight in the air, stop in his tracks, hee-haw one time, and never lift a hoof more. His eyes would turn upside down in his head, and no matter the time of the day, he'd stand frozen stock-still till the sun would go down and he was taken to his hay.

Squire Didapper was a man of command and not often disobeyed. So the mule was a sore point with him. He had called in the best vet, who inserted a tube just below Redbone's tail and blew hard and strong, till Redbone's eyes turned right side up and he pulled plow in his old wonted way.

It was a fine thyme-scented day, and spring plowing went steady as Redbone and twelve other mules and two yokes of oxen pulled plows all around. Redbone was in the Buckfield, a square of stumpy and stony new ground. The mule was not happy with stones and stumps and stopped at his plow, still as death, stock-still in his usual way, mule ears standing straight up, and his eyes turned upside down in his head. There the Squire knew he would stand in his tracks till near sundown, and it was not yet even close to midday. The vet was not at home, but Didapper knew that Dolphus, though an humble man, was a man of many skills. He knew mules even better than bees.

So off ran a servant to fetch Dolph straightway. The servant found him smoking his old reed-stemmed pipe and singing

> *Boil them cabbage down, boys.*
> *Turn them hoecakes round, boys.*
> *The only song that I can sing*
> *Is boil them cabbage down.*

and mending an old black wash pot all the while, at his blacksmithing stand. He had great columns of pipe smoke thick round his head as he hammered and hummed.

Dolphus finished his blacksmithing job and went on his way, singing a tune. When he reached the Squire's, old Redbone was standing stock-still, his mule ears straight up, and his eyes turned upside down in his head.

Dolphus inserted the tube just below his tail with kicking and trouble just as the expert vet had done before. Then Dolphus held the bridle to pull, while the Squire was to blow. The Squire put the tube to his mouth and blew, and he blew, but was too weak in the wind. Again, he blew and he blew, but could make no headway. Old Redbone stood frozen stock-still with his mule ears straight up and his eyes upside down in his head. "You puff hard on your pipe," said Didapper to Dolph, "so you have more wind in your chest than me. This time I'll pull on the mule and you come back and blow." So Dolphus obeyed and exchanged places with Squire. But instead of straightway blowing away as Didapper expected he would, the first thing Dolph did was to pull out the tube and turn it around and put the other end in.

"Why damn ye, Sir," said the Squire, as he wiped sweat from his brow with his monogrammed hanky from out his silk vest just by its golden watch chain. "After all of that trouble and kicking and swearing I had to get the tube in!"

"Why damn ye, as well," said our Dolphus. "Ye must not think that I'll put the same end in my mouth that you had in your own."

For indeed our Dolphus was an humble man, but a man of many skills, and a man particular in his own way. Old Redbone at this broke into a loud braying laugh so hearty and hard that the tube was not needed again. From this very time on, his mule ears always lay flat and his eyes stayed right side up in his head just as they should. For each time he'd see old Didapper take his monogrammed hanky from out his silk vest just by his golden watch chain, and shake it out with authority and an air of command, he'd think of our Dolphus, and the plowing went easier and smoother, and even through stones and a stumpy new ground.

XV

The Fool Killer: A Fable for Academics

~ ❧ ~

Nature still defeats
The frosty science of the cloistered men,
Their theories, conceits.   —Vita Sackville-West

Lowell Beecher had a humpback and, some said, a chip on his shoulder as well. Beecher thought of himself as the resident Fool Killer, and he served a large radius around. In his superiority, he lived to himself, measuring and sorting, prying and judging—reducing the puzzling to the point where science could get a firm grip and hold tight with the rein.

The neighborhood called him Horseapple, and sometimes Crabapple behind his back. He had the longest grey Puritan face, thin and sharp. His tongue was as smart as a whip or a sting. With a profile like a hatchet and a disposition to match, he was cutting sarcastic as Voltaire, and just as venomous sour, the sour of a green June apple in May.

"Horseapple," said Davy-Joe, as he encountered him trudging up the muddy red-clay road toward the country church one Sunday morning. "Why are you in so all-fired big of a hurry?" Horseapple always looked like he was in a bigger hurry than he was because of his hump and the way he had to trudge along at a forty-five-degree angle, as if he were plunging straight into the progressive future like an arrow.

He gave Davy-Joe a look from the top of his short-sighted eyeballs as if to say, "Don't fool with me, or talk any fool talk, or act in any fool way, or I'll be obliged to kill you right here and now." If looks could kill, Davy-Joe's toes would have pointed up and he'd have been outstretched in the road.

While Beecher considered Davy-Joe a damfool, the fact was that, although not book-learned and simple, he was smart enough in his own way. He never lost sight of the whole by belaboring the small, and his vision was keen. So he quickly saw his mistake in engaging Horseapple at all. But on this fine day, Davy-Joe was in a brave and peckish mood. He had had a big breakfast with the wife and the young'uns—a breakfast of ham and grits, and red-eye gravy too, topped off with smoking-hot buttered biscuits, big as saucers, and new-made fig preserves. Besides, after a long soaking rain, it was a clear Sabbath morn, bright as a bride or a new baby's face, and he looked forward to church and seeing us neighbors and friends. He said cheerfully with his usual frank, open smile, "Horseapple, how are your symptoms segashuatin' this fine Sunday morn? What a frog strangler we had last night. I've never seen such a flood on the river since I was knee-high to a butterfly, and our batteau, with me in it, got washed out of the bulrushers plumb down to Alston Depot, and I had to call on a buzzard to fly me back home to my mam. What a ride I had, and I could see the world from his dark buzzard wings in the way Noah did from the ark 'fore the dove."

Horseapple started not to answer such damfool talk, but instead, after long painful pause, condescended to say, "Sir, I believe you borrowed more than the buzzard's wings when you were knee-high to a butterfly. I deduce from the sound of it that you borrowed his brains as well, and use them to this day. There is not one ounce of sense in a word that you say."

Well, Davy-Joe had been called simple—and rabbit-brained and lame-brained and pea-brained and guinea-brained—before, but never buzzard-brained, and this made him a mite more peckish and set him a bit on his edge. Beecher took his friendly nonsense and twisted its tone into serious mean. Such intentional meanness took away Davy-Joe's frank, open smile.

"Buzzard-brained I mout be," Davy-Joe replied, "but I ain't narrer-wasp-assted, as is some that I knows."

Well, Beecher had been called Crabapple and unfriendly, and cranky and mean, but never narrer-wasp-assted before, so his own bristles rose and his edge got sharper than a hatchet or arrow whetted to point on the finest grindstone.

"You better clar my way, or you're one more damfool I'll just have to kill." He gave Davy-Joe the look of a con-stipated Descartes or Voltaire, then trudged on by, resolute to be on his way, to strive and labor, to reduce and to mea-sure, to sort and assess and explain and to do.

Davy-Joe contemplated dulling Horseapple's sting by

tanning his narrer-wasp-assted hide, but just as he did, a little whirlwind picked up leaves from the path and set them to spin. Beecher, with eyes fixed as usual close at his feet, did not see; but this was not lost on Davy-Joe, who watched it dance by on its way, gazing at its slow spin as if put in a trance. Deep in his own heart of hearts, Davy-Joe knew it was better to leave Horseapple alone. For unlike old Beecher, Davy-Joe's way was to stand ready to hold what the world would give, and then accept and receive, rather than shape, strive, and pry and to do and to force with his will. And Beecher, besides, had been known, in his own sneaky way, never to abide what he deemed damfool talk, or anyone acting damfool, or, most particularly, fooling with him. No, Davy-Joe, who knew he was simple and ignorant, was far from a fool, and so let sour old Horseapple pass.

Now Beecher was not heading for preaching as was Davy-Joe; they were only by coincidence walking the same way. And since, as we see, Beecher was not one to suffer converse with fools, he walked on ahead leaving the latter behind, and Davy-Joe let him go. Yes, they walked the same road, but alone, single file, with length of three wagons between. To Davy-Joe's simple mind, the back of Beecher's old rusty-brown coat, and his skin-and-bone arms working with elbows thrust out to each side, looked just like a hornet or giant red wasp, mad and mean. Bent as he was, his narrow black-trousered pointy old tail through the prongs of his too-tight claw-hammer coat indeed stuck out like a wasp getting ready to sting.

As the two walked along on the muddy clay road, the clay stuck to their boots like sweet-gum resin, and Beecher grew near a foot taller as the clay caked thicker and thicker on his boot soles. Davy-Joe looked to his feet and stomped to knock his off, but noticed that Horseapple did not. He just kept on trudging straight ahead like a laboring, slow-motion arrow, and getting more worked up and caught up in the resin—and taller and taller by the step.

When they reached the yard of the whitewashed clap-boarded church, Davy-Joe could not resist a comment to his friend, Big Biscuit McJunkins, arriving there at the same time. "Look there at old Crabapple. With the clay on his feet, I swear he is almost grown tall enough to be a whole man."

This was overheard by Beecher himself, who now made up his mind to kill both the damfools in a double fool-killing spree. Now all that was left for him was to reduce the problem to the certain details of just how, where, and when. He already knew he'd be the *who,* and gladly besides.

Davy-Joe and Big Biscuit turned in to the swept dirt yard of the church; but Horseapple, with a frown like he was sucking a lemon picked green off the tree, and flinging a last sarcastic barb about churchgoing damfools, kept trudging along like a Voltaire walking astraddle of briars or an old barbed-wire fence.

Now Davy-Joe and Big Biscuit were easy enough targets for an expert Fool Killer like Beecher. Both men, although good-natured and charitable and easygoing, were not learned in the books. And they were spacious of soul but, truth to speak, not spacious of brain. Big Biscuit, it was said, had once shot at a target with an unloaded hoe-handle, and Davy-Joe had thought Shakespeare some kind of far-off jungle book with the natives at war. They both loved a fond fiddle, their wives, and their chaps, and could gaze at a fire on their hearths late at night for hours on end with no thoughts in their brains clean a-tall. This bothered them none in the least, not a-tall. They stood as God made them, poor ignorant sods, ready receptive to hold what the world would bestow and with hearts open wide to receive. They prayed for God's mercies and welcomed His mysteries unchallenged besides. Unlike Beecher, they had read neither Bacon nor Descartes—which for Beecher was a death-sentencing crime.

Yes, if looks could just kill, Horseapple this fine Sunday morning would have already many times over killed them both dead.

The congregation now assembling outside the old church's doors was discussing the crops and the weather, new babies, who among them was sick, who was well, the old folks, the neighbors, the shut-ins, and such, on and endlessly on, so Horseapple perceived. They were friendly and easy and open and kindly, talking what Beecher would call foolishness lightheartedly each one to each beneath a pair of ancient, great sheltering oaks that spread from the church to the graves of the elders of yore, joining, bonding, encircling them all. Davy-Joe and Big Biscuit were joked with and bantered, joked and bantered themselves, and with no ill or harm done. No poison injected, no feelings stung; and they, like all gathered, were set honored places in the midst of the neighborhood ring.

Horseapple, with his brown-coated hump and sharp pointed tail, buzzed and droned with his grumblings, and frowned with his sourest green-apple, lemon-pursed mouth about damfool wastes of good time. He particularly held the religious as pious great fools, the kings of them all. As for himself, his god was God-Science-Reason, and he worshipped at shrine every day. Mystery and deep mumbo-jumbo he just could not abide. Complexity he dispensed with by dividing right down to the bone to the simplified, specialized grid that his mind could then grasp and conquer and comfortably hold. He went on his way, arms jerkily working at angles akimbo like a meat chopper at work at his great bloody board. In his best bent-forward walk, his pointed black tail stuck straight out from between the prongs of his coat, indeed, as Davy-Joe had thought, like a great laboring wasp preparing to sting.

When he trudged to the top of the hill in his mud-heavy boots on his way, the first notes of their song came faintly to his ears through his grumbling mumble of drone. They sang:

> *Shall we gather at the river,*
> *The beautiful, the beautiful river?*
> *Gather with the Saints at the river*
> *That flows by the throne of God.*

Hadn't these damfools had enough of rivers and floods and mud-caked shoes? A river was just one more obstacle to cross—like one more mystery to solve, or one more riddle (like a plague) for man to strive to be rid of—a confounded nuisance that should be drained, dammed up, or bridged fully o'er. No reason to gather at a fool river's side, if not to get cross. He saw then in vision of light: with enough accumulated knowledge of dismembered parts, nature would bend pliantly to enlightened man's will, and enlightened new man would run shining utopian world—but for the likes of undammed rivers and fools. And as for Saints, sainted damfools, more the like. Superstitions all, powerless before God-Science's sway. Such superstitions were the folly of children of woods, rivers, and fields. He droned on with his grumblings, scowled with his gaze at his feet, and trudged on. He would have to get home to Descartes for dark solace by lamplight, to clear out the taint of this ambiguous mush from his brain.

Now Beecher had traveled and indeed Beecher knew books. He had read his Voltaire and his Locke, his Bacon, his Denis Diderot. He had studied intently his complete Jean Jacques Rousseau, had looked into Hume, Newton, and more. He was always observing with shake of his head the absurd superstitions of all the damfools who had not. These ignorant rubes who sang about rivers and Saints, and fooled away time with their fiddles and banjos, with their reels, jigs, and songs, who sat about hearths for hour on hour with child on the knee and no thoughts in their brains clean a-tall, weaving their fictions and telling their tales of impossible feats and the like, who gathered together before Sunday's church doors discussing the crops and the weather, who was sick, who was well, the neighbors, the old folks, and more—all these he considered High Criminals of Mind, deserving a painful, long-lingering death at a Fool Killer's hands. Extermination of their lot would do the earth good, like fleas taken from dog. Indeed, their damfooledness was a capital, a killing, offence, and Crabapple just waited a chance and a way to pronounce a blanket death sentence on all.

When he met up with Davy-Joe this morning, he was traveling back home from the town, where he'd lodged in one room for a week while he read at the local athenaeum of books. He had been rereading his old friends, the French Philosophes, refreshing his memory and getting inspired to fit out the theme for a great book he had made his life's work. Now trudging toward home, he was anxious to get under way with his tome, and to do. Away from his desk a whole week, he was eager to work with his notes, to reduce, and divide, to set down, to categorize, and explain, and to do and to do.

He was writing his great encyclopedia, in the very manner of his beloved Diderot: *The History and Theory of Fooldom Through Time,* and from *A* straight down to *Z.* There was nothing he scrupled not to enter—inquisition of empirical Truth was his holy pursuit. It was now in eighty-six volumes and growing apace. He was just down through cataloguing *Q.* Like his view of the workings of the world, he granted priority to the parts over the whole, to the measured and sorted, all reduced to the simplified small that the mind could control, feeling smug and comfortable at the end.

The home that he trudged toward was no home for him, for only his work and his mission were home, were allegiance and life. The place that he occupied was place with a chair and a desk, an inkwell and shelf. The pleasures of Home—and a Place and a Church—were the things talked of most by the fools he'd just left, and that kept them in ignorance far from books and things of the mind. His own home was Science, his career, the realm and the kingdom of mind. In his *History and Theory of Fooldom,* he entered Home, Church, Neighbors, and Place just neatly down under *H, C, N,* and *P.* For his method and format were pure Diderot.

Enlightened he was—an angel of light—and he scorned all were not. He inhabited a land of Voltaires and Rousseaus and, if left to him, would never place foot on the ground. These fiddling damfool neighbors around all had grits for brains. Those who gathered with Saints came from caves. And he'd written them all in his book with coldest great glee. He had named them by names. His crooked brown back had gotten more stooped as he inked in their names; and his bony old black-trousered tail through his too-tight claw-hammer coat had grown more pointed each night passed to day.

He had taken some pleasure in using a phrase from their Bible as epigraph to his great labored tomes. *The letter killeth* blazed in big red letters on his book's title page, intending the words of St. Paul in a way St. Paul would have never approved. And this made Beecher happier than a dung beetle in dung. He underscored his epigraph with vigor and venom that imprinted the line on subsequent pages within. He smirked over the appropriateness of this with a bitter grimace, for each word in his work was intended as poison-tipped arrow to kill all damfools who wasted their days, gathering by rivers, open church doors, and their hearths where they fiddled good time away.

Now under *B* went Big Biscuit and under *D,* Davy-Joe. Under *S* went the Saints, under *H* went the Hearth, under *N* went Neighbors, and under *F,* Family; and he catalogued them all with Reason and Order of scientist's skill. His subjects were making a great knowledge nest like the wasp's—each categorized in a chamber and cell. He labored all that clear Sunday night by the meager lamplight of his own chambered cell, building his lonely wasp's nest of science because he'd so much to record, so much to reduce, so much to tell. He built his great nest each cell at a time. As he did, his writing grew cramped with the strain, and his right hand grew knotted and bumpy and gnarled.

His pen, it was dipped in the poison of wasps, and though Davy-Joe may have been a damfool, he was once again right in his way. Beecher did look even more like a wasp as he worked at his desk, on the nest of his book in brown too-tight old coat and sharp elbows outstretched, twitching and scratching with pen.

So hot at his work this night and day, he had forgotten to eat except for the single cold biscuit he'd packed from his breakfast in town. And he didn't even remember eating the biscuit at all, so rapt he was in the cloud of ideas and his vitriol mission to do and to do—to kill with his letters as many damfools as he could in a night and a day.

Monday dawned bright, as splendid a sunrise as God ever made, but Beecher missed the grace of the morn, lying in bed. The sunlight burned his eyes through their aching closed lids. He had exhausted himself and spent all his sap through the night with the wasp stings of his pen.

And now to his ink-hungover brain, what a jar to the tender and delicate mind that had just been imbibing the liquor of Science with the likes of Descartes and Voltaire to hear from outside his window and door the raucous mule-braying of Big Biscuit and the ass-braying of his pal Davy-Joe. They had learned at church on the day just before that old Comer lay sick at the very same time when his crops needed gathering in. So the pair were just out on their way to help with the harvest in their sick neighbor's fields. They were chortling and joking like two mindless magpies as they passed with their tools on their shoulders and full knapsacks with dinners on their broad farmer's backs. From their nonsense of talk he discerned through the chatter of fools, "I wonder if old Horseapple's alive."

"He don't make no sound from inside."

"His symptoms must segashuate porely today."

"Too many tedjous small things and no fiddle to play."

Big Biscuit just pointed his heavy unloaded hoe-handle straight at Horseapple's door to emphasize who and where he described.

But enough of these fools. He'd suffer them no more, and with this, once and for all, he'd end their fool play. In his Science-based view of the world, he'd advance his big plan here and now and without further delay. A giant grey hornet's nest, two papery head-thicknesses wide, grew great from a limb by his desk's open window that day. It had been growing in size now, tiny cell at a time, for years as his only companion and neighbor and friend, waiting, it seemed, to serve in a neighborly way. He broke it a-loose with one whack of his long schoolmaster's pointer made from the branch of a stunted horseapple tree—aimed trajectory meant to fall down its hypotenuse right square in the tracks of the fools where they lifted their ignorant pilgrims' feet on their way. The hornets by thousands were riled and packing the venom of combined deadliest spiders and adders and scorpions stored in their tails and made lethal by many a moiling in cells of the dark of a nest on a hot August day.

But the nest, which had no knowledge of Euclid's geometry, in breaking loose, hit the spring of a branch at the window, which shot it straight back at Crabapple. And it fell squarely on his bony bald head. Well, the scene was not pretty, and accompanied by screams. Big and Dave could not help, for old Crabapple's door was bolted, as was his usual distrustful, unneighborly way. Till they broke the heavy old door down, it was too late. The pair got a few stings of their own, but mainly just stood silent in honest amaze at the mystery of how it all came to be. And Horseapple's symptoms segashuated now in no way a-tall.

For the Fool Killer was killed, stung to death, with his shining, new-sharpened pen still sitting alone in its clot of dark ink, still sitting alone to this day in deserted stale cell—his death another thing to explain, a puzzle and riddle unsolved by the neighbors to this day. And churchgoers still sing of their rivers and Saints, and gather outside their open church doors, just to talk of the crops and the weather, who is sick, new babies, the neighbors, Horseapple's death, and such and some more. And among them still gather Big Biscuit and our good Davy-Joe. And still as they do, great rivers run, and leaves are caught up in soft whirling winds in their usual way. Taletellers go on telling their tales. And still fiddlers bow on and bow on, and their elbows never tire, or get worn out from the desk at the sleeve. And fools by their glowing hearth fires will for hours still sit, just to gaze and to gaze, with a child on the knee, and no notion to riddle, reduce, and to do and to do.

XVI

The Miller's Cat: A Story in Which Just Nothing Happens a-Tall

~ ❧ ~

Nothing keeps its own way more than the river.
—Wendell Berry

"What fools these mortals be!" exclaimed Tranquilla, the fat old tabby, fat with mice, as she watched the miller long and long. In fever of sound and fury, the miller worried all the day about everything that signified to cat wisdom just nothing a-tall. Even if the great wheel were to come to a halt, he'd still live on. The river would not run dry in its bed.

Her mind off men, Tranquilla watched the dance of the flour dust sway and hang suspended, rocking in the rays of the sun. It soothed her brain and reminded her of catnip and cheese. From the motes in the sun, her lazy gold eyes turned to the motion of the great water wheel. This was good for an hour as she listened to rhythm and gurgle and splash, and gazed charmed at its turn. Like her, it was happy to sit on its pins and go nowhere a-tall. It ended where it begun, like a dance, or the turning of day into day, of summer to winter to summer again. The rhythm of water turning the wheel was the rhythm of life. And this she knew well.

Yes, the wheel was her friend and she purred as it hummed. It stayed fixed in its place and took on the moss and was content with the musical water that fed it from trace.

Her cat trance turned to a catnap and snooze, and she dreamed then of warm milk in the winter and new-cut cheese in the fall, and of golden bright leaves that whirled in the wind. Mice she hardly dreamed of at all. They required her to run.

On this warm spring day, she had spring fever for sure. Even in her dream, she just slept. She dreamed that she dreamed; and in that dream, she still slept.

The miller soon woke her abruptly with the clatter of work. He and his sons were sweeping the floor. She was roused to change place. Her pink mouth gave a yawn, smelling faintly of cheese, and she moved to a bright sunny sill, where she settled and again took her ease.

There were birds in the bushes, birds in the trees. She watched and she watched, with no impulse to spring. Life was fat and was lazy, to be lived as she pleased. The mill wheel rolled on, on its watery way, still fixed in its place, and, like her, never thought of a move.

Farmers came and they went, bags on shoulders, casks and barrels on wheels. The wagons rumbled noisily over the cobbles with their iron-clad wheels going home from the mill. Horses clattered their horse-shoed hooves on the stones. Hobnailed boots rang loudly about. They brought in the corn, took home their meal, with the aid of the wheel. They came and they went, but the mill wheel stayed put in its comfortable groove. They came to the wheel. And the wheel—well, it never took one step to them.

Yes, the wheel was her friend and her twin. She curled up round in a ball and looked just like him. And her bright tabby gold in the sun, lying round on the sill, also looked like the big golden orb of the day. Then at night when she curled on the sill in the moon, in its silver she looked like the calm, satisfied orb of the night. She quietly blended in place both night and day, and in that she took justified pride and delight. Miller, with his silver and gold orbs turned into coin, went off on his way in the dusk. But she always stayed. He quickly, abruptly, took off in his wagon with lurch and a jerk, but she was always quick and contented to stay. Yes, contented to stay.

Day turned to night, night into day, and the cat lived on smoothly with nothing to spend, nothing to pay. At night, with all mortals far gone, she moved only to dance when the fiddle was played, as she heard it far down in the valley, from the banks of the river below. For a dance was her pleasure; it reminded of wheel. You turned and you spun but always came back to where you'd begun. You had nowhere to get, and pleasured in standing in place. It was almost as much fun as chasing your own bright tabby tail.

The miller neither danced, sang, nor played. He was too busy with meal. He reminded cat of an arrow, flying sharp at a target for aim. He was more like the wagons that had places to go, more like the coins that passed hand to hand, more like the iron-bound wheels of the wagon that were restless to roll. The world required bridges to get them across, place to place, and traveling head foremost in line, aiming daily at targets ever distant, unknown, ever new.

Instead of wagons and bridges, targets, arrows, and coins, the sun and the moon and the wheel were her own beau ideal. They merged close in her windowsill world, dream in dream.

And still nothing happened a-tall each day into day. Nothing to spend, nothing to pay. "But it does not creep in petty pace," Tranquilla flatly declared, for the day was enough, and the sun on the sill. This place was her home, and she loved it right well. She never imagined a wider, or smoother, a warmer, or different sill, or a pleasanter mill in which to dream, dance, and dwell.

XVII
Croton Oil

~ ❧ ~

As Cousin Killdee stood by the man-high potbellied stove in his country store, he unraveled his tale. With the backdrop of shadowy, well-stocked shelves crowded with their motley array of general merchandise, farm necessities, and curiosities—*notions,* as they were called in earlier days—he took center stage, as he spoke in his usual unhurried, deadpan way, his rich voice a mellifluous monotone bass that somehow magically never resulted in the slightest hint of tedium. His back to the fire, with hands crossed behind to the warmth, he struck unselfconsciously an orator's pose, as he faced his assembled audience of gallused farmer neighbors and friends seated around the old stove. Out of the shadows over his left shoulder projected the rack of a nine-point buck he and his sons had killed many years ago, the dust of time upon it; and beyond it dangled strips of brown molasses-coated flypaper, still there from the summer before. Over his right shone galvanized-tin foot tubs and assorted buckets and pails hanging from wires and bent nails. With this familiar homey background, and the more or less undivided attention of his audience, he began:

"You know my pap was the agricultural agent in these parts, and folks came to see him with all manner of questions, seeking all sorts of advice—often beyond the knowledge and wisdom an ag agent was licensed or even likely to have. One particular cap he was most often forced to wear was the vet's. Lacking a real one around here, and a free one anywhere, Pap was put into round places his square peg couldn't fit, but he always tried. Folks expected it of him—as their local man of science with that white magic of degrees tied to his name like a cow trailing its tail.

"This particular day, Reuben Lee Jeter, a dairy farmer from just over the hill, came to Pap with the problem of animal blockage. It was near the end of a long day, and Pap was tired and in a hurry to go in to Mam's supper. 'Well, Doc' (they all called him Doc though he was none—neither medical nor otherwise). 'Well, Doc,' the dairyman said in his low countryman's drawl, 'she's blocked and belly swollen with pain. No bowel movement in Lord knows how many days. I'd sure take it kindly if you'd give me advice.'

"This was an easy enough one for Pap, who had experience at physicking the equine and bovine kind. His ag agent and countryman's knowledge sufficiently covered the case at hand—or thus he thought. Croton oil would do. It was the potent laxative of choice in rural ways, for people and animals too—the mighty emetic that packed the power to loosen a Gordian knot or move hardened concrete.

"'Well Reuben Lee Jeter,' he said, 'you just take a full large glass of croton oil, open her mouth, and put it down her throat. Make her take all of it to a drop, and sure that will do.' With that, Pap called it a day.

"Pap went on about his business, wearing the cap of weather prophet one morning, marriage counselor the next, and Reuben Lee went on his way, to dose his blocked animal with a full glass of croton oil—nearly a quart—to be forced down her throat, all to a drop.

"It was several weeks before his and neighbor Jeter's paths crossed again, and Reuben Lee had not been over the hill to stop by in his usual way with questions to pose to his 'Doc.' When his eyes met Pap's, they didn't look at him straight, or bear quite the same old trust and confidence sure.

"Pap, who was good at sensing people's moods, often before they were aware of them themselves, registered this right off, and noticed Reuben Lee had a kind of hang-dog and embarrassed look on his cheek. Looking kind of sheepish, Jeter, well known as you know for the gift of the gab, for once did not know rightly just what to say.

"So Pap, remembering the subject of their last meeting, aimed to pick up right where they had left off, and asked in his usual bluff way, 'Reuben Lee, how'd that blocked animal do? Did the croton oil do the trick?'

"From the corner of his eyes, Jeter looked at him with a look of great hurt and a little dismay and said that he didn't just rightly know. 'Well sure, I did exactly as you bid, made a glass of croton oil, nearly a quart, held open her mouth, and forced the final drop in, and the blocking problem was fixed, and that is for sure. But the cat ran away.'

"The cat! Pap's jaw fell slack open. He'd thought dairyman Jeter had said cow 'stead of cat. After a bit of a pause to gain back his feet, he questioned Reuben the outcome, with some fear and trembling besides, 'Well, how is the cat?'

"'Don't rightly know,' was reply. 'Haven't seed hide nor hair of her since. Last time that I did, she was flying and had three cats with her too. One digging, one covering, and the other scouting for ground.'

"Whether or not Reuben Lee's tale of the four cats was all totally true, we'd not know rightly to say. But the cat never came back—whether physically unable, or out of pique at her master, or clean out of fear.

"Pap gradually regained the neighborhood's trust, but had gleaned a great lesson from it all. He learned that before dosing or giving advice from his lofty high perch, that no matter the problem or how piddling it seemed, he must listen right down to the letter and take it all in, no matter how tired or how busy the day, or how good supper smells from the door. And that a cow man could have other than cows."

The old stove glowed red, and on this farmer's wet and sleety holiday, full bellies shook with good humor all around and greying old heads nodded at wisdom perceived. The folks put up their feet, ate bologna and saltines and cheese that was cut from the hoop, and with other such yarns, tall and true, many a belly once again shook, as they passed off a winter's cold day.

XVIII
Fair Grace by the Eddying Pool

~ ∾ ~

*For in ancient Mesopotamia, the river people held the
fish to be a symbol both of fertility and great wisdom.*

The quiet little neighborhood by the great river's
banks depended a lot this time of the year on what folks
received from the great river's deeps. It was too warm this
time of the year to be butchering hogs, for the meat would
not save and the hams fail to cure.

But this year the fish were not there, or withholding
themselves if they were. Fish traps failed—even the best.
The men with their poles caught not even old shoes. And
all this, for a time, caused a great minor stir. "What will we
do for our stew?" the grannies asked their daughters all
around. "Fall won't be fall without proper big feasts at the
end of the day." They wondered and wished, they fished
and they puzzled and fished and surmised, then put all
complaints and their puzzlement away with their fish traps
and poles. This year there just wouldn't be either fish or
fish feasts, and so that was that. Sometimes it happened
that way. And exactly why, no one could say. No one was to
blame.

Tow-headed young'uns, old enough to remember from last year in the fall, told their mamas and grannies about, "My belly is needing a great heap of fish stew to be happy again, and the nights by the fire coals a-singing and a-talking of fish." But the grannies all said, "Hush, child. Never mind. Go on. Do your chores."

The daughters and sons puzzled at their work off and on in the day, of something they missed, then remembered it was the feasts that were held as ritual that time of the year. Like the plowing, the planting, laying by, the picking of apples, strawberries, pomegranates, and figs, or the making of scuppernong wine, these feasts marked the time of the slow-passing, circling year.

They asked all their mamas and grannies around, "Ain't it time for the fish?" But the fish were not there—or withholding themselves if they were.

The folks by the great river's banks worked on in their usual way, and sat by their hearth fires these cool autumn nights to gaze and to gaze at the fire coals with no far-reaching thoughts clean a-tall—that is, beyond occasional notice of having no fish feasts this year clean a-tall. Wonder, then acceptance, the pattern it went. "Well, that then is that. We will just have to wait for the hams and the hogs."

But the hogs were not fattening just as they should. The acorns had been scarce this year in the woods. The surplus of bright orange pumpkins the hogs usually ate had not made on their shriveled-up, yellowing vines, and neither had squash earlier on in the year. "We'll just have to take up a notch in our belts," the men looked to each, smiled half-heartedly, and shook solemn heads. The cupboards grew emptier. In the pantries, spaces showed dark between bright shiny jars. The young'uns asked questions; their elders replied, "Hush, child. Never mind. That ain't for young'uns to know. Go on. Do your chores."

For these were mysteries even for grownups, and for them to accept and not know—and especially not for the chaps, with their chores left to do.

Still the river flowed on, rolled over its rocks in its shallows, polishing stones on its way, fell down its falls, where men built their mills, grew deep and deeper in its lengths of straight channel and banks, and sometimes paused shortly to eddy quietly in pools.

There was one particular great round eddying pool where a fair young daughter of the river came to sit and sing songs and think deep and think long. The eddies reflected the thoughts in her mind. As she watched leaves spin golden in a soft whirling wind that mirrored the swirl of the pool, she eddied a plan, and there on the banks did the deed.

She took the leftover wool from the family's sheep, spun it round and around with the leavings of honey-gold flax and the ruined brown cotton that had been discarded away. To the rhythmical whirr of her fast-flying wheel and the cadence of song, she spun three great spools of bright thread, golden as corn silk or sunlight or the locks of her own flaxen hair.

She sang "Bobry Allen" as she plied her fine golden thread with long supple fingers soft as the thread that she wove, and as smooth as the silk she had only once seen.

> *It was in the early month of May*
> *When the flowers they were blooming,*
> *Sweet William lay so very low,*
> *In love with Bobry Allen.*
> *He sent his servant through the town.*
> *He sent him to her dwellin'.*
> *He cried, "My master's very low,*
> *In love with Bobry Allen."*
> *Then rose she up to go to town,*
> *Going to his dwelling.*
> *While she stayed, this is all she sayed:*
> *"Young man, I think you're dying."*
> *He turned his face unto the wall,*
> *Busting out a-crying:*
> *"Adieu, adieu, adieu to all.*
> *Farewell to Bobry Allen."*
> *She turned about to go back home.*
> *She heard the death bell tolling.*
> *She looked to the east, and then to west.*
> *She saw the corpse a-coming.*
> *She cried out loud, "Lay down that corpse*
> *And let me look upon him;*
> *For I might have saved this young man's life*
> *If I had owned I loved him.*

Oh, Mother, go and dig my grave,
Dig it long and narrow,
For Sweet William died for me today,
And I'll die for him tomorrow."
Sweet William died on Saturday night,
And Bobry Allen on Sunday.
Her mother died for the love of both.
She died on Easter Monday.
There they three lay in the old churchyard,
Side by side a-sleeping.
Green briar grew from Sweet William's breast
And a rose from Bobry Allen's.
They grew till they reached the old church top,
Where they could grow no higher.
There they formed a true love's knot,
With the rose around the briar.

There on her plaited-cane chair by the river's steep banks at the eddying pool, she sang as she wove a great net with the best skill she could, a great net that the sunlight made gold, gold as the words of her song. The net was soft and light as her hair and almost as fair to behold. The wind played with it as it floated from her lap, and her hair blew out in mirror behind. The pool eddied on, while the breeze played tricks with the net and her hair.

She talked to the wind: "Tangle it then! Well, just straighten it out by yourself." And on most occasions, the wind listened and did.

Fair Grace worked on with her golden great net, for Grace was her name, and fair indeed was she to behold. Many an evening she would slip to the river's still banks and the eddying pool when her day's chores were done, to sit and to sing as she wove. Each rib of her net was a family, and she named each by name. And she and her naming and songs and the fast-flying motion of fingers on wheel were such as to charm waves of the river to rhyme. Her songs and her motions and river grew one.

"Had I a golden thread," she sang, "and a needle so fine, I would weave a magic strand of a rainbow design."

Then near the new-ripened harvester's moon, she finished her weaving and threw out her great golden net with the help of the wind to the hollow and depths of the pool. She then turned her back, and went on.

In the homes of the river folk, cupboards grew bare. The pantries' dark spaces between bright shining jars grew wider each day passing day. On some shelves, the jars were all gone.

A niggardly harvest had turned barren dry. Folk woke day after day to a tinder-dry world, when the sun was hateful, when even the cattle in the sparse autumn fields caught common fear.

The hogs were still too lean to butcher and the young'uns started whimpering as their tight, sunken bellies growled for the right kind of food. Ashcake and hoecake and cornbread were all of their fare; and the ashcakes and hoecakes and cornbread grew small and smaller and

fewer and few. Though they feared, those by the river stoically took all in their stride. They would take, then, what
came, and would starve if they must. With strong souls
they patiently awaited new day and what new day would
bring. And how often their eyes searched the west for a
sign, for clouds or a flash of the lightning harbing'ring
rain.

In the dead quiet heat of the day, Grace would often go
to her eddying pool, sing ballads of old, and gaze long and
gaze longer with no far-reaching thoughts clean a-tall,
while the cupboards grew lighter, and darker the spaces
between bright shining jars, while the ashcakes and hoecakes and cornbread grew ever smaller and fewer than few.

And then the day that all the pantries grew empty but
for one bright shiny jar—and the next-to-last ashcake
smoked on the hearth—and the children all whimpered
and their tight bellies growled—our Grace came to her
eddying pool. She had grown to a woman in this season of
want. Her figure had ripened despite the lean times. She
came to the river but to sing a sad song and to gaze at the
stream. It was in and about the time of the great heavy
hunter's moon. And in its bright amber light, its new ripe
fullness reflecting her own, our Grace beheld there her
great golden net in quick motion alive and sparkling with
great amber fish. The river had answered her doing and
trust, with doing now of its own. She had woven her best
into song, thread, and net, then had waited in peace and the
quiet of soul. 'Stead of wringing her hands, she had used

them to weave. With an eddying soul, she was always pre-
pared, always ready, to give, and receive.

Yes, just like her net, she'd stood ready to hold what
the river would bring. And the river had answered her back
with a net teeming amber with fish, great net full enough
for a thousand gold feasts that would feed all the folk on
the river's bright banks. They would bring back the round-
ness and glow to all gaunt, sunken cheeks.

The stewpots of neighbors were made ready now, and
they bubbled up round and full to the brim. Coals glowed,
friends encircled, and full tow-headed young'uns sat with
satisfied round bellies around. Fiddles rang out. Banjos all
hummed. Old ballads were sung. Fond old stories were
told, told again, and retold. "Tell that one again,
Grampaw," the young'uns implored. And sure it was done.
And fair Grace was among them with bright flaxen hair,
singing her ballads, the wind in her curls, and was noticed
for first time by many to full manhood just come.

XIX

Spindleshanks at Ballylee

I'll be talking after my death.
—Peig Sayers, Gaelic teller of tales

There was a staghorn sumac growing in Tyger's green glen just down from Ballylee. Its twigs were so plaited, and its leaves so many and as thick as the hair on the head, that it made quite a roof from the rain, better than cedar or cypress or slate or the tin. Under its branches on this dark stormy day stood a singer of songs who took shelter from storm on the wind. The rain drove on strong through the swirling grey mists, but the singer stood dry as if charmed. The slender bright leaves had a mind for his greying old head and its thinning grey strands.

"This old thin grey thatch," said the singer of songs to the leaves, "no longer shelters this pate from the storm and the scorch of the sun. I get stronger in soul but ever thinner in hank and leaner in shank with the years." Our neighborhood had recently, in good-humored jest, picked up his own playful name for himself. "Spindleshanks" we called him, for tottering he was, and uneasy on legs that were powerful once at the plow, and expert, supple, and good in

137

the dance. Now he felt like a tattered old coat on a stick—stick dry and bent from a gnarled hawthorn tree, not smooth and supple as the sumac's own twigs that resembled the silky soft horns of the stag.

All his family and friends had preceded him crossing that far-distant shore, and he was alone by the Tyger's bright waves except for some few old acquaintances, friendly enough for sure, but neither his blood nor close. So Spindleshanks turned his bright blue flashing eyes inward and spoke to the kindly green sheltering bush, having no one else before him in whom to confide soul to soul.

The bush answered right back with a twinkle of leaves and sometimes a touch of his arm or his cheek with a twig, whose velvet was soft as the down of the stag's new velvety horn.

Now today in this great tossing rain, the storm lasted much longer than usual, and the mists swirled much thicker, more ghostly, and much closer to head, but the bush kept old Spindleshanks dry and protected his old tattered coat and his old balding head. So the singer of songs made verses to give his humble kind shelter fair passionate praise. Slender branches waved and rocked in time with the wind and Spindleshanks' rhythm and rhyme, for the branches and leaves never before had verses like these made expressly for them. And these lines were so passionate, thankful, and kind, for old Spindleshanks sang with great force and clapped with his hands the more loudly for each year of his age. The bush knew he meant what he sang, that the song came from soul. So its branches swayed on, as in a great trance to the chime of his rhyme. Its leaves danced in tune with his lines. As it did then, its branches pleated and pleached ever closer to make the old man a hat, and a cloak to cover his ragged old coat. The raindrops on leaves were slowed from the chaos of storm and entered themselves in the charm. They danced like the leaves in tune with the chime of his rhyme and turned their channeling paths from his head. They wet all the ground with their muck and their mire, but old Spindleshanks' feet under thick sumac bush stayed planted on driest of ground.

Two brothers driven from plow by the storm stood in the door of a far-distant barn. They looked down the hill to a glow in the swirling grey mist of the green-sheltered glen. It was nothing but bush, but in the dark of the storm, it shone with a silver halo all around, like the silver of Spindleshanks' head. They looked, looked again, and then peered at the glistening silver and green in the middle of storm. Fat pelting raindrops the size of birds' eggs hit them full in the face even standing in barn, and the pellets struck like ice balls that peppered and stung. Their clothes were all sopping, and their feet were clogged heavy with mud.

But there in the glen, they could see as clearly as day paltry old Spindleshanks dry as a mouse in his warm nest of hay. They were only mildly amazed, for old Spindleshanks, as they knew, always could either sing up, or quiet down, a storm. At least so it was said by all of us around—for, as all of us knew, Spindleshanks had true gift of the song.

Country wisdom had taught us the three major gifts of Almighty to men. The first was strong principles of truth, then next was the dance, and the last was charmed poetry's song, singing-master to body and soul. Spindleshanks had all three, at least in his time, though for dancing his once-supple shanks were now weakened with age. The storm soon abated, and the day moved its way to a close. Spindleshanks went unsteadily home alone to the ashes of a solitary hearth, and the boys played rough play of jostling and knocking each other from the path as they made it on home to supper and chores.

Now several years later, and Spindleshanks had borne his poor stick of a body to a rest in the grave. The same little brothers, now about to be men, passed the same sumac bush in the misty green glen on their way to the plow. On this day, however, they stopped sudden and frozen amazed. For the bush's light leaves issued forth the bright tune of the passionate song that old Spindleshanks sang in its praise. The leaves sang in chorus the most beautiful, enchantingest music that ever was heard. They sang of the dance and of ancient charmed tunes and true principles too, and the three merged as one in the rhyme of its song. The leaves sparkled with sunlight like raindrops or gems and danced in the gleam of the glen, and danced like the ripples on deep-flowing river below.

The boys stopped their banter and play, and stepped off a stately dance like two healthy young stags. Their heads they down-turned and made as to cross them like velvety antlers or velvety branches of bush. The clicks of the branches in song were the touch of their antlers that met. Their feet walked as heavy as hooves and their legs spindle-skinny with youth like the dancing young fawn, and, beginning to fuzz like a satyr or faun, wove their way like the branches and trunks in the great ghostly forest around. The song magically awoke the senses of young, yet, when heard by the passionate old, became singing-master to soul.

But when the music all stopped, as did dance and the glow, the boys walked their way as if nothing had happened, to their plows at the top of the hill. There with their feet firmly planted in newly plowed rows, broad legged they stood to survey the strange kindly bush that had danced and had sung and had lightened their way. Around its bright circle of light, as they looked, there then stood a woman as fair as the dawn, all dressed out in white, and whose skin was so white it was blue. Then as in a blush, her face looked just as luminous clear as the blooms of a spring apple tree—clustering blossoms through which sunlight luminous falls—or then pink like the luster glowing inside of shells. She was walking quite slowly in circle in rhythm of song, and taking the cadence of music the bush had just sung. She was first just herself, then showed old Spindleshanks' form, became herself once again, and then finally turned three times in a twirl and was gone. The brothers stared at each other—again stood open-mouth amazed. And after a pause and a hearty deep-chested laugh, they snorted like stags that are startled in depths of the wood. They then set their legs to the plow, boy's legs that over the newly turned soil of their fathers' own fields grew stouter and sturdier, stronger and steadier each day as they walked, as they shuffled their feet in Spindleshanks' dance and sang Spindleshanks' passionate songs on their way.

XX

The Cure

As the sleet fell with its peppering sound on the old store's tin roof, the gallused men drew a bit closer to the potbellied stove, whose sides were glowing cherry red from the oak and hickory blaze. The wind occasionally got caught up in a drainpipe or discarded Coke bottle and made a low and mournful moan. "The voices of the dead," old Caleb said from his bench close up to the stove. Old farmer Lyman recalled one long dead, as his memory was triggered by the store owner's recitation of a recent indiscretion of one of the community's own. It seems that this fellow named Bonnie Dee Peacock, who was too much addicted to drink, had finally hit rock bottom. He had had a bad wreck and nearly killed his fool self. When he got out of the hospital, his city kin took him to one of those fashionable drying-out places, then enrolled him in one of those ever more numerous and lucrative establishments— clinics, so called—for the growing legion of alcohol and drug dependent. He was a hard case. Bonnie Dee wouldn't

143

be cured. He'd go on the wagon for a time, then fall off, as the expression went. He was now trying AA but not finding a cure.

The men around the fire talked sincerely of remedies, for Bonnie Dee was one of their own. And even though he was a trial, he had his good qualities; at least he'd shown them at fleeting times before he'd gotten so out of control. These good times had grown fewer and fewer, and now he was never his old self—only a trouble to his kin and to the neighbors, who mused on his fate. They riddled and thought, wishing they knew what to do and could come up with a cure.

So it was in this rather solemn abyss that old farmer Lyman told us his tale out of the long time ago. Seems that one of his own kin way back, by the name of John Phoenix, had the same weakness as Bonnie Dee. He was a well-respected farmer, of some prominence in the community around, but would take his drink or two. The two soon became three and four and more, till things got out of hand. As a drunk, John Phoenix was neither noisy, messy, nor mean and remained more or less responsible through it all. It was in this way that he was tolerated, though regretted by his fellows around. If Phoenix wanted to choose this as his way, regrettable as it was, then he had the right. Some closest to him tried to help and suggest, even trying a remedy or two, but to no avail. He wouldn't be cured.

Another piece of split oak was placed through the hinged iron door of the great roaring stove, as Lyman began now in earnest to spin out his tale. The store's three resident dogs lay stretched flat on the floor between the assemblage with noses straight out, but eyes upturned and alert to take it all in. They knew from the pace and rhythm of talk that for some long time they'd not be disturbed, not have to mind heavy brogans and boots on their paws or their tails.

Old Lyman resumed: "Even though we were just knee-high to a tadpole, we children around knew John Phoenix had plumb disgraced himself. As the old folks were wont to say, we didn't have to eat the whole cow to know we had a piece of beef. It was just in the air, in the hushed pitying tone of the voices of neighbors and kin. It was known to be true in the shaking of heads and the look in the eye. But, yes, sad as it was, John Phoenix had the right to do as he did. He was a gentleman, sober or drunk, and always behaved in his quiet, respectable way.

"He'd ride his fine bay horse to the village, where he'd soon drink his fill, then come back on home in the deep of the night. His horse knew the way and the reins dangled down to its side. John Phoenix would sit, more or less erect, though his head would be bowed, chin on chest, chest to chin. He sat his horse as solid as when sober. And this went on. His wife fretted and worried, but gave him his way. He'd always come in, undress, half hang up his clothes, and fall in his bed to sleep it all off.

"One starry fall night, he didn't sit his horse as firmly as he usually did. His timing was off or he'd had extra too much of the good harvest season's good cheer, and he fell off the horse, dead drunk by the side of the road. His horse, it ambled on back to its stall. Some of his hands from the farm, in the joy of a harvest well done, also returning quite happy from town, were driving on home in a one-horse wagon. There they found John Phoenix unhurt by the side of the road, sound asleep on the ground, his still-hatted head resting on crook of his arm. They straight picked him up and stowed him in the wagon behind and took him on in.

"Arriving at the farmhouse's backyard, the hands were then greeted by John Phoenix's wife, Minnie Sue, who came out to the porch in her flour-sack gown. The hands told her what had occurred. 'Ma'am, he's asleep in the wagon, like a baby asleep,' they all said. Miss Minnie, as sober and practical as ever, replied, y'all let him remain, that the cool of the morning would help bring him to. Here, he'd sleep it all off. So she went back inside to her goose-feather bed to continue her sleep, and the hands went to tether the horse and to their cabins straightway. The farm settled down and returned to its accustomed quiet and calm. It was as silent as the tomb.

"Just before daybreak, John Phoenix stirred and began to awake. The moon had gone down and new-flown clouds were hiding the stars. It was dark as only a dark in our country could be—as dark as the proverbial tomb. He shifted and turned. Reaching first to his left, and then to his right, he encountered on both sides the cold of planed wooden walls. Reaching up, he felt the cold wooden seat of the wagon just over his head. Then flashed through his mind the night in the town, the ride back toward home, the falling, and no horse neath him now. He'd had a calamity sure and was dead and now buried alive. His cries raised the house, his wife, children, and all. His yells roused the bunkhouse and tenant cabins around. They were heard all the way to old neighbor Cornbread Boyer's, and by all his big brood. 'Help, help, I've been buried alive.'

"The story of John Phoenix's burial and borning again went the rounds to be sure throughout the whole land. It was told time and again, near and then wide. Cold sober, he was, cold sober ashamed. His gentlemanly luster was tarnished by amusement, and sometimes ill-mannered laughter, in ways that his serious drinking just never did. In this, and his fright, John Phoenix's burial occasioned his cure. Those of us who had known him had said only death would cure him from drink, and sure it was death indeed that gave him his cure.

"Phoenix stayed on the wagon, in manner of speaking, for rest of his days. He never fell off in remembering the night in the wagon in his pitch-black backyard."

The common-sense crew round the stove stayed in silence a good while after Lyman had finished his bittersweet tale. They let wisdom sink in as they focused their eyes on the hypnotic cherry-red glow of the stove. Then proprietor Killdee knocked out his cold pipe in a measured and formal, slow pace, like the holder of gavel in solemn proceeding of meeting or court. This broke the charm of the mystery of telling and was sign it was now time to get up and stretch and to move.

The hounds were the first to sense this and stirred themselves up well betimes. They were waiting to see what would be the next move for the day. A hunt perhaps, or a walk, or, drat, just another deep tale.

From the circle at the potbellied stove, John Phoenix's old story went out and drew breath of new life, cross three-quarters of century again. Its tones blended with all the ghost voices in wind on that sleety cold day. He'd gone long ago to his grave, really this time, and breathed and drank no more. And though his passion and his frailty, his grief and love of life all now were spent, his memory remained, all on the way of the truth. What would his successors in this place come to make of him now, and how would it go with their own Bonnie Dee?

XXI
Sídhe and Ingus

They who travel, seldom come home holy.
—Thomas à Kempis

When folks see swirlings of leaves in their paths, they know that the wind is alive with a will. They stand still in silence to watch as the whirling moves by in the summer red dust. This was a fine and a perfect hot August day for such swirling of leaves. The land was all dry and the leaves of the trees were rumpled and ruffled with wilt. Some had yellowed and fallen already as prelude to fall. Late corn in the fields had roped-up dry leaves, pointed like spears. Grass and weeds all around had collapsed on themselves in the solemn high disc of the August red sun.

Sídhe (they pronounced her name Shee) stood mopping her brow with the hem of her apron at her open front door. She was dressed in a light cotton print that had pictures of full heavy grapes and red-purple pomegranates. Now Sídhe loved the breeze, as it cooled off her neck, as it blew her long locks from bare shoulders and cheeks. She loved the fair wind off the eddies of rivers and the banks of still summer pools. She was fair in love with wind as it rose over trees.

Fair Sídhe was also in love with a lad just above these same trees. She often pictured herself as the wind making free progress to his humble house door. But more than the trees stood in her way.

For Sídhe and her lad, whose name was Ingus, like the wandering amorous fellow of yore, had been told by stern fathers to stay far and away. Their families were as different as fire and the ice, of hot springs and snow, and of night and the day. On mountain he lived, and she at the spring at the foot just below. She could look at his light, he could hark to her lamp; but only the wind on their lips could kiss each to each.

Sídhe loved her Ingus enough to take flight on the wind and never see family more. Bold Ingus, the same, met Sídhe secretly in wood where the crags of the hill made sad melody in wind. Their lips needed no breeze this time to kiss each to each, so they vowed their decision to go far away over river, valley, and hill, to mate soul to soul, to wed high to low, mountain to spring, earth to wind, fire to snow.

They grieved for the places they'd leave, for the accustomed fond paths in the woods that they roamed. They would never have these for their feet to touch ever again, never see the light brighten yellow in east from the window or door, or see it set red in the west from the table filled full beneath mother and father's kindly old hands. For kindly they were, only stern in this single command that forbade.

Sídhe and Ingus, on the morrow's deep midnight by

the heavy late August moon, were to meet at this crag of the hill and fly forth like the wind to a stranger's new land beyond river and hill.

They grieved all the day, touching for last time all that they loved. For Sídhe, it was hearth, its pots and its pulls, the place family gathered, the spits for the roasting young rabbits and peanuts and chestnuts and young brother's snare-caught birds. She once hugged her brother, who found it quite strange. But he hugged her right back and looked puzzled when she turned quick to go. Big tears filled her eyes, but these were not seen.

Through their blur, she watched as her mama sat peeling her apples in white, fragrant curls. Her ma sang the old songs as she peeled, the ballads that Sídhe herself learned and had sung with her beautiful clear voice since a girl:

I left my dear father. I broke his command.
I left my dear mother, a-ringing her hands.
I once loved a young man, as dear as my life.
He often has promised to make me his wife.
His promise he fulfilled; he made me his wife,
And what have I come to, by being his wife:
My husband a drunkard, I sick on my bed.
He's always a-grumbling; and I wish I was dead.
Young ladies, young ladies, take warning from me.
Don't place your dependance on a green growing tree,
For the leaves they will wither; the roots they will die.
A young man will fool you, as one have fooled I.
They will hug you and kiss you and tell you more lies

Than cross-ties on a railroad and stars in the skies.
I'm troubled. I'm troubled. I'm troubled in mind.
If trouble don't kill me, I'll live a long time.
I'll build me a mansion on the mountain so high
Where the wild birds can see me and hear my sad cry,
Where the wild birds can see me and hear my poor moan,
For I am a poor girl, and a long ways from home.

While her mother sang these sad strains, Sídhe looked at her great tabby tom oblivious to all, as he made a gold ball on the threshold of door. He lay with his back to the road. For tabby had taken just that place and no more. No one could dislodge him, and it was hard for Sídhe to go in or, most especially, go out.

All her feelings were acute and for the smallest and humblest of things—from the comfortable impress of her chair as she sat at her place at the table for this her last time, to the fond feel of the curve of the great silver spoon that she worried the last of her last supper with, in the house of her birth, the only dwelling that she'd ever known. She looked long and long at the grease turning grey into tallow on supper her mother had labored all day to provide. Even the cinnamoned apples of great crusted pie could not draw her attention away.

The shadows grew longer and soon she would light the lamps of the house for the very last time. Meanwhile, Ingus, not really much more of a wanderer at heart than Sídhe despite his name, shed his own tear or two over sister and mother and Pa and his mule, not to mention his cow, his beagles, his setters, and fyce. He had worked in the fields till his supper was set. He had lit then the lamps and saw them mirrored way down mountainside in the lamps that his Sídhe herself had just lit. He imagined her there in her pomegranated dress, her arms lit by lamplight, and forgot then his tears.

He stole from the house singing snatches of song:

I know a valley fair, Eileen Aroon.
I know a cottage there, Eileen Aroon.
Far in that valley's shade
I know a tender maid,
Flow'r of the hazel glade, Eileen Aroon.

The silent old moon rode her car to the top of the hill; and their households asleep, the pair made their way to the crag. Sídhe of wind and Ingus of earth were to wed on the morrow and live far from the homes that they loved. There was no other choice at their feet.

He reached the crag and waited. While he waited, he sang a sad old song of bitter partings and bitterer finality:

I'd rather be in some dark holler
Where the sun refused to shine
Than to be home alone, knowing you're not my own.
That would drive me out of my mind.
So blow your whistle, freight train.
Take us far on down the track.
We're going away. We're leaving today.
We're going and we ain't coming back.

The moon grew dark with great hairy clouds like locks

blown in the eyes, as Sídhe met him at the crag and they commenced on their way. The wind rose high in the trees and rubbed branches like dry bones in mournfullest sound. Sídhe loved the winds, yet was fearful of these. They sang her a ballad of deaths, and she would have feared had not Ingus then guided her down the dark cliffs of the crag, his hand in hers.

Then the torrents of rain fell their way. The trees rocked with the weight of the wind like sea waves in storm. The parched earth that had opened in cracks with the droughts of the summer now rejoiced in the rain. The earth that had once seemed to hold its breath as it slept in the drought now seemed to awake with a sigh of relief and a great mighty yawn.

Still the trees rocked like sea waves in a storm, and torrent-drenched and slippery stones of the crag made dangerous descent. It slowed them, but safely at last they got down.

They walked all the night through the rain, that poured heavier yet. They were drenched to the skin, but the rain was a warm August rain and only resulted in slowing them down. It could not stop their journey to make them as one.

With the morning, they walked hand in hand to the plain. The plain was in flood and the river so high they could not get them o'er. The bridge to the pass, when was finally reached that rainy midday, was washed totally out, not a plank left on plank or a pole upon pole, and with no one around. Had the bridge just been there, most surely they'd have been on their way.

But Ingus, who had wandered this path from his plow a few times before, knew a zigzag of stones where the red men of old had impounded the shad and sturgeon and speared them with stone-pointed spears. To Fish-Dam, as was called, they then came, still drenched in the torrents of storm, and the water had covered the stones. Ingus remembered the place of the stones, so led Sídhe by the hand and they found the bottom of rock with their feet.

Ingus was broad-chested hardy, and Sídhe brave and game. In both glowed the health of the land. So they started the long crossing, hand once again held in hand. The current was swift and the billows pressed hard like the waves under gale in the sea, and Sídhe was swept from the zigzag of stones. Her element was wind and not wind-driven water in flood. And Ingus was earth, and like soil he was also swept helplessly far down the tide. They washed half-alive to a small island downstream, which they shared with the beavers and minks, the 'possums and coons, even snakes made docile by this dire extreme. Mice lay half-drowned by the side of the snakes; foxes and rabbits each other beside. An old johnboat batteau was lodged high in a tree.

Sídhe's kinfolks lived close to the isle, and the cousins were out on the river bluff doing chores of the day, taking time to rejoice in a tinder-dry world of brown ruin turned green. They spotted the pair from their fields up above and brought them to shore with a batteau and pulley and chain.

Much to the cousins' surprise, there was Sídhe, one of their own, in company of the scion of a family unknown. Both sets of their parents were called, and forthwith the next day arrived with the brothers and sisters and grandpas and grandmas in tow. It took six sets of wagons to garner them all.

And here they all gathered on green ridge over banks of the great ancient ford of Fish-Dam, where the fish, ages past, were impounded and speared and the ancient ones gathered to eat their great ritual feasts—gifts of peace and content that bonded their tribes and their families to one, and anchored to place.

The cousins were wealthy in fertile, rich soil and many fat hogs. They had corn for all critters and left plenty corn beside for their big copper still. The enemy families, brought together in shared dire flesh-and-blood cause, had been frantic with worry when Sídhe and Ingus were missed in their beds the next morn, and their paths to the crag pointed certain to death by a fall. So in joy of relief, both sides put their feet now beneath communal great table that groaned heavy with plenteous food—meat, meal, and molasses, and the fish of the flood—and balmed all their wounds well enough to dip and to sup from out the same bounteous bowl.

The jug of corn passed around, the fiddle and banjo from shelf, the rifles uncocked and at rest on their safe mantel crotch, the night drew on merrily to close. Beds were made all around, and pallets of star-pointed quilts for the young. The two warring families settled, and drowsed, and dropped off to sleep one by one, and under one roof at last slept as one. Their snores made one symphony as under a single great maestro's baton. And harmony reigned.

Sídhe and Ingus were married and lived exactly halfway between their mas and their pas, their brothers and sisters and kin, just halfway down mountain on the way to the spring. Sídhe of the wind and Ingus of earth raised up a big passel of young'uns to sit on their grandpas' stout knees, to ask for the story just told and, still never tiring, to hear over and over and retold once again, till they drifted to sleep, the tale of the night when it stormed on the crag and the river flowed high and washed out the bridge just to give them a home and this tale.

XXII
Stories for Christmas, or Willows Like Wands

~ ∾ ~

Stories bind the people into the land. —Barry Lopez

The sad dark eyes of the gypsy children shone in circle round the gypsy campfire. The young sat mostly in the shadow of elbows and hips, quietly watching, taking things in. This had been the third move in as many days and the travelers were seeking willow, knew where willows were, but had not yet reached the riverbank where the trees grew in abundance, luxuriantly, like laurel or olive branches to make crowns for the brows. The willows were for baskets, their stock in trade. They would work the pliant reedy stems into magical forms, phantasms of wood, shapes out of the imagination pure. And these shapes of the mind would soon bear food, and produce, and clothes—shapes to hold the world, for them and their own and the great world outside.

The traveling people carried their shapes with them in mind, and their craft in the tips of supple fingers. Men and women cut, men and women cured, men and women wove. The suppleness of fingers mirrored suppleness of wood.

When the willows gave out, they moved on. It was as if their shapes and their craft used up the world. In their big arcing movements, in rhythm to motion of stars, they would pass here again, years down the road, and the children at this campfire would then have babes of their own. And the willows grew back, replenished, like the eyes of the child, emptied by sleep each night to hold then the new world of each day, like the baskets they made.

This wagon-bound band stayed to themselves. Their fires stumbled upon in the night by the world outside produced what seemed a lurid strange scene, something from outside the nailed down and fixed, outside the stable of their light and their day. The dark faces lit by the hues of the fire, reflecting in eyes like the deer's, would remain in the minds of these viewers and give them sharp pause in their light, turning the cogs of their minds like the creaking dry wheels of the trio of wagons that carried these wanderers on their silent sure way—willow driven, with want of the willow—with the willows like wands magically commanding them all.

It was in and about the shortest day of the year, when night came early and stayed long, and there was less light for willow cutting and weaving and more campfire time to sit and listen and muse. The children knew of the outside's Christmas, now few days away—of the dolls and the toys and whistles and drums in the houses that sat and did not move. Though they kept to the shadows and umbrageous groves and the paths unseen, their peregrinations sometimes brought them to edges of towns, quickly passed on their way. It took only a moment for the alert dark eyes of the young to take all of it in. There would be children at play, and called in to supper, walking up heavy stone steps where the glow of multi-bright-colored lights shone from windows with sparkling trees, the glow of these lights making water-color stipples through glass on prism-bright faces aglow with their rowdy loud play in the cold. Their hot breath steamed round golden-curled heads like holiday wreaths, as they went in to tables and hearths. And the dark gypsy children saw all between curtains' closed fringe. Toy soldiers, toy drums, rocking horses, and more.

Dark eyes watched the scene in a world quite as strange and as distant to them as the moon. Toy guns and pianos and whistles and dolls. Though gypsy children knew there'd be no visit from Father Christmas for them, still they could hope against hope. In place of a chimney or door, maybe a wagon or ashes of campfire would do.

At blazing bright campfire now, they asked about the toys and the dolls and the drums. One little girl walking by wagon today had looked up to see, straight in her path, a little blonde girl holding by one arm the dangled figure of doll, with hair as bright and blonde as her own. Black eyes reflected in blue and they passed on silently, each turning to gaze.

This was a question for the elder. All eyes turned to him as, like gentle Father Christmas himself, he opened his venerable pack and unraveled his words. His pack was the great deep cave of his making that issued like river in flood in the shapes of the mind.

Around gypsy fires this cold Christmas Eve, there would be stories for Christmas, to be carried much longer than dolls caught by the sleeve. In his familiar, comforting tones, the elder told his listeners once again the story of magical trees.

"Down by the shallows of the silver still river," he began, "and in the deepest dark wood that we wandering people call our ancient home, there once grew the supplest and straightest, tallest bright-green willow trees, with leaves in the sun as silver and sharp as great spears. When one of our people cut off a branch, next day in its place there'd be two. So we stayed near and were not forced to roam. These magic willows were like wands to the soul. They shaped themselves of their own volition into baskets, into Amalthea's horns. They made carts and wagons and houses for men. Men sat in them, slept on their mats, shaped them with sighs. Over all, our people gathered together under them, and the great willow wands swayed as in blessing in the river's soft breeze.

"The people gave thanks to the willow and to Maker of willows and men, and kept humble serene. We never would seek the paved paths of the world or the silver and gold of its way, contented with the gold and silver of leaves. And the branches were wands to make magic bright shapes of the wood—alchemy best, oldest and true. This was our people's tradition and grew long from the richness of soil in the shallows of stream. All this was in the long-ago time before the evil befell, and the great silver willow was cut at its base and could never regrow. It was then we were cast on the road."

So ran the elder's stories, one after another connected, deepening the mystery of time—tumbling this night like bright toys from the limitless pack of his mind. Turning over each package wrapped with the tinsel of time, the children unwrapped them with minds made supple with magic and joy. Then each following night at the fires, he bestowed them—each after each, each for all, and each child would unwrap them to find its deepest heart's purest desire, doll for one, drum to another, toy wagon, toy horse, whistle, or charm. The wand of the willow held in elder's kind hand made miracle shapes for his children, making sense of the miracle of day, and that lasted much longer than toy soldiers and drums, or the houses and pavements of men.

XXIII
The Golden Cup and Bowl

The modern dogma is comfort at any cost.
                                          —Aldo Leopold
We all prefer comfort to joy.   —Flannery O'Connor

"Son, where's your raising? Get up and give Odell your chair." This was spoken to Rob-Emmet Cullen, one of Hamp's tow-headed, cotton-top young'uns, as a neighbor stopped by for a neighborly chat. Hamp and Rob-Emmet were sitting in great cane-bottomed rockers in the brush-broom-swept yard, taking a leisurely sit-down after a satisfactory morning of work and a big midday meal. Hamp's round belly was tight on his belt as he sat in his chair. "'Bout to cut me in half," he said as he loosened it a notch. "If her cooking gets any better, I don't know what I will do."

Rob-Emmet got up obediently to give Odell his seat and began to play with the hound that lay lazily cool under the steps of the house, for it was deep Carolina summer, and hot.

The ladies of the place had cut dogwood switches, tied them together with old calico strips, and swept all the yards clean of grass and leaves. The stone-bordered paths were as neat as the furrows Hamp plowed. This was the time after the crops were laid by, and there was less now to do until the harvest began to come in. Now they were doing the fill-in jobs—work that was not dictated by weather or time of the year. This was also the time of their church's Big Meeting, and revivals all around. The special churchgoing lasted five full weeks. And there were visitors, kin, and preachers staying around at all the family seats in the close neighborhood.

And such was the topic of conversation between Hamp and Odell. "Old Preacher Bullen has been exhorting the wicked to give over their sins of the flesh. Precious few of them I has nowadays," said Odell with a chuckle, but looking a bit wistful, as if to suggest he would like to have more. Now Odell was an extragood neighbor, and always with a twinkle of devilment in his electric-blue eyes. He was always good merry company and wise. He never failed to have a new story on someone, never to hinder or harm, but one that would sum up the subject's character to a tee. He was naturally interested in folks, and the nature of the astonishing things that they did or that happened to them. "Human nature," he would say, "is a wondersome thing, and more amazin' than the seasons, themselves wondersome enough."

Hamp quite agreed and waited for the story that must inevitably come.

Odell settled comfortably into his storytelling pose as the great cauldron of fable and tale simmered and boiled. Today, he was of more serious a mind and Hamp could tell already that this tale would be an unusual one and one whose depths he might not plumb. Odell would do that to him occasionally when the mood was upon him. This morning Odell had seen ravens and crows, a red-tailed hawk, and even an eagle high in the sky. The ravens and crows were ominous signs, and the hawk and eagle were bringers of messages from across the line. It was probably the last that had brought him the tale.

The story was about a poor old woman who came to his door. She was alone and the worse for wear. She was cast out in the world and had no place of her own like so many of their own farm friends and families these very rough days, these "raven days" as the folks all round had begun to call them in their want and need. Like a spirit, she wandered, unquiet, over these dusty red-clay roads. He had seen her before, but she'd never stopped in until now. A bit distracted, she seemed as if addled from shock and storm. Her heavy man's shoes were sadly worn, and the hem of her dress, which was once beautiful and rare with flowers of lace, was now tattered with long and rough wear. A briar had taken its toll here and there, and the mud had spattered it sore. The lace that remained was yellow with age.

"Well, Auntie, can I help you?" Odell asked with respect, but dreaded hearing a yea.

She answered with young eyes that greatly belied her age. "Thank you, kindly," she said. "It will be help I'll be requiring of many, and help that will not come easy, and from some not at all till the last."

"Then why do you wander about? Have you no place of

your own?" he asked her with candor, a straight look in her eyes, as blue as his own.

"I had borne me thirteen children fair and strong. I labored for them, and they for me. And before any of them were full grown, all were taken from my side, and my thirteen fields which each was to have. My children all still live, but poorly, barely, yet they are kept from me by force and cruel law, and my eyes cry themselves swollen each night as I sleep."

"And what of their fields? Are they plowed, and by whom?"

"My children's fields are taken by strangers who divide them for spoil. The strangers never care to plow them, for to them sweat is a curse, and a sad dishonor is the tilling of soil. So my children are ensnared and have all that is rightfully theirs taken away, and I am turned out of door, to walk these red-clay roads as if I were a tattered old crone or the ghost of a ghost. And that is why you see me here, so shabby, and wandering, woebegone, no place to call my own, my children orphaned while their poor mother, turned out of door, cries her eyes to swell them shut each fitful sleep the kind darkness brings."

And still the ragged old woman was no beggar. She would have died rather than beg. It was clear that she had once been a proud lady of high standing and at one time as noble as queen. No queen was she now, but a lady for sure. Yes, a lady for sure.

Odell, like most of us, was busy with his life, getting

and spending, pleasuring and being responsible too, paying Preacher Bullen, hosting Big Meeting, and all that, and would rather have had the old woman away. He already had an aging mother in his care, and here was yet another helpless old dear who needed to lean on the young.

But much in this woman showed strength through her rags and her age. Her eyes were so keen and so young, as young as his own. He had strange fleeting thoughts that the leaning might be his if she deemed him worthy to enter her world and let him do so.

She held him with the power of her gaze until he broke the deep trance and then asked, almost demanded, it seemed, "Lady, what help can I give? I'll pour you fresh milk in a bowl and give you my new wheaten loaf."

"'Tis more than food I will require," she answered him straight. "It is I who would spread bounty for all—to those who're made to wander from their homes, to all my children kept from me. I would nourish the soil of my own children's fields, in bondage now held, and depleted full sore by usurper's deep guile. No, food it is not I require."

"I have some golden dollars. I am more fortunate than most, and I can spare you a few. Will you then take these?"

"'Tis more than dollars I require. It's I who'd bestow great silver and gold to those who must wander from homes to beg from out a stranger's hands. It's I who'd give great wealth to all my children kept from me. No, gold it is not I require. Instead, I would have it to give, for riches are mine, of sky and the soil, if reclaimed."

"Well, I have fame and standing in the world—respectability. I host Big Meeting and the Reverend too and have position with the law and in the town. The merchants know me, and some even fear. Important people ask advice and do my bidding every day. If I told your story, you'd have honor back and not be walking in tatters and rags."

"Do these eyes look downcast, honor-lost? I'm not ashamed, for my dress is honest poor. I've not relinquished virtue a jot. No, 'tis more than fame and standing I require. It's I who would bestow standing in the world to those who seek it now in devious, less than honest ways, foreswearing and belying their homes. It's I who'd give great fame to all my children kept from me. I'd nourish with the strength of heritage fine. No, fame and standing it is not I require."

"Please tell me then, fair lady of the rags. You hold my eyes with eyes so like my own, with gaze that cuts me to heart. If you withhold, begrudge me truth, I'll never be happy more."

"You were not happy when to your door I came, nor are you now, I see. You miss and lack your own. For you are oldest of my children born. They took you from me small; they tore you crying from my arms when only four years old. They locked me in a cell in chains, kept me without a chair to sit, or darkness then to sleep, despoiled my house, and burned it all. They only left us eyes, they said, that we might weep. For these sad years I've still been in their chains. And you, my orphan son, have you had omens none?"

"I've dreamed many a night of lady dressed in silks of richest blue with heart so wide as sky, a noble lady straight and tall who, head held high and eyes uplooking to the sky, did not forget her children, who to her were all in all."

"My son, you bring again the tears to these red swollen eyes. I cry for you, my child, taken from your mother's silk-clad arms by hateful arms in scratchy wool of blackest blue that bore the fateful lightning of a terrible swift sword."

"And this, then, Mother, this, the place I live, is not my home? The books I read to children on my knee, the clothes in closet, talk I hear, songs sung, not my own?"

"Your fields were taken when they burned them o'er. They took them for their own. Then the years, for one so young, erased the memory and shame of deeds they'd done. And with the guile of serpent tongue, perverted from the rightful heirs, the truth of what was taken then and how. The books, the clothes, the songs, they then are truly foreign to your soul."

"And you, my mother, you my greatest, saddest loss. They took the mother from the son. And here I've dwelled an orphan long, not knowing rightly of my loss, but filling lack as best I could with getting, spending, pleasures, gold, and food and fame, respectability. Ah, Mother, true, I must know all, though knowing might now blast the eyes. What can I do; what must I know?"

The question hung so sadly, seriously on the midnight air, that all the world stood silent as it seemed, awaiting words from lips of tattered lady standing in the door. For with the look of monarch, she had turned to leave, a parting mother to her orphaned son.

"I have been loved," she said, "had been loved by many in my time. There have been those who bled and those who gave their lives for just a trace of these lips' smiles. They deemed me worthy of their passion and their blood and gave me all they were. They gave me more than food and status, gold and fame. They gave up all of self and all they wished them ever to become. They placed their passion in my golden cup and bowl, and it's on that I've fed in chains, in cruel prison and exile—when food and fields and fame were gone. And it's from that I have my strength today to seek my orphaned children out, and call them home to their own fields—my orphaned babes, precious each and all, who do not know their mother loved, and loves, and always will remain to love, to give her all. . . . So it is passion I require." And reaching in her ragged and mud-splattered cloak, she then brought forth a jewel-crusted golden cup and bowl, and placed them gently in her listener's trembling hands. And then was gone without a word.

With this, Odell ended his tale.

"Well hell," Hamp said as he opened the shells of boiled peanuts expertly with forefinger and thumb, and popped the salty goodies in his mouth, "you've done it again. What does all that talking mean?"

"Blessed if I know," said Odell back. "It all came in a dream. Just pass those peanuts this way here, and then let's us just take a snooze. They're fitting out our farmhouse later in the day for central heat and air. I know I'll need to get my nap before they come, with bother and their noise."

Rockers stopped rocking, and all then fell silent, but for snores. But little tow-headed Rob-Emmet, tired of playing with the dog, had lurked within the golden circle of the fable-cauldron's boil and heard strange story's every word. He pondered on it long and well and riddled and reriddled night and day, year passing into year. With memory's clearer eye, no strange old woman then did he see, but young lady fresh in bloom with walk of queen. And when he grew a man, turned from off his father's fields by alien culture's way, he sought and found this same lost lady's cup, and filled to brim with all his soul and passion up.

XXIV
Amalthea's Horn

Harlan had a goat named Amalthea. She was the biggest, fattest, best-cared-for goat anywhere thereabouts. Her shaggy flaxen coat was long but never allowed to go matted with beggar-lice or cuckleburs or weeds. Her horns were great spiral affairs that lent regal bearing to her simple goat head. Now that the children were all grown up and gone, she was Harlan's great pride and joy. He petted her as much as she would let him, and almost as much as he did his lap dogs and coon dogs, bird dogs, beagles, and hounds, and even his favorite little yappy fyce.

Harlan was a caution, both he and Amalthea. The two would be seen together in pasture and field, like two children at play. Wherever Harlan would go, there would be Amalthea. Harlan's wife, Sally Pat, milked her, and she gave the creamiest milk, which made the very best cheese. All Harlan's babies had been raised up on these. His five sons had grown up happy and sturdy, and steered a mean plow as straight as a longleaf pine. They were gone now to

172

nearby fields of their own. His five daughters were peart and bright as new tacks, with great ready smiles. They also grew up healthy, steady, and sturdy on Amalthea's gift. They had all chosen farmers for husbands and had raised large bounding broods, fed from the milk of Amalthea's kids, given by Harlan for their own.

Amalthea's milk was the sweetest and mildest anyone had tasted in town. The people marveled and swore it had hint of the honey, and reminded them always of the nectar of flowers or sweet sugarcane. "Ambrosia," they called it, fit for a king. "What was the secret?" they asked each to each on their way.

No amount of gold could buy her, they knew. "No thank y'all kindly," he'd say, "don't reckon I'll sell." So they'd just have to spy out the secret from Har, and then mint more goats like Amalthea to have for their own, on a goat-minting machine. What a business they'd make, and what prices they'd bring. Great visions of smoking Amalthea Milk and Cheese Factories gleamed in their dreams and crested the hilltops completely encircling the town. But they traveled a lot and did famous things in the world, so put off the mission for this time or that.

Then during a lull in their travels and big doings in the great world outside, the people got serious about their mission to spy. It would be a quaint diversion at home in this time they were bored. So they sent first a simple-minded young lad, who could honestly play innocent, to ask not so innocent questions and learn something this way. But this

did not work, for the lad forgot what little he'd gleaned
and got mainly confused and confounded by all the attention,
and all going on. So they next sent a man of aplomb and
renown, Traylock Triggerfoot by name, to ask him right
out a straightforward "How!" This worked even less, so
paraded six more jet-setting Triggerfoot corporate types,
with various stratagems, one by one, in different worldly
ploy and most cunning guise. They too got just nowhere
a-tall.

Then came scientist-geneticist Prof. Traylock
Triggerfoot II. Degreed as he was and strutting the part, he
was farthest from getting the truth but, as old expression
went, was closest to getting our Harlan's goat. Pardon the
pun. "More degrees than a rectal thermometer," our Harlan
declared as he summed up the Triggerfoot scene.

Now the people all around had sure enough got their
curiosities up. For a time, old Har was as interesting as
Paris, Cancun, or L.A. Eccentric old Harlan and his sometimes malodorous goat had become the riddle and in-game
to puzzle and play—and by far the most common talk of
the day. They tried and they tried by every means to figure
it out, but got no help from Harlan, who had rightly begun
to wonder what was up. He had grown greatly suspicious
with the trooping of town on his place one by one in a
stream like a great solemn Macy's Thanksgiving Parade.
They'd not done it before. What was his Amalthea to
them? Or them to Amalthea? Why interest so great from
those who spun round the globe in a day? No, they had

never been so before. Pastures and their creatures had never before been an interest for them.

So spying was next. They would watch the goat's every move, follow it wherever it went to find out the secret that made her milk sweet. Now this plan had its problems, for there was old Har, who was goat-devoted too. How could they spy unbeknownst to Harlan's keen eye? They solved it by keeping their distance far up on a microwave tower on hill and took shifts with scopes and binoculars throughout the day. After the committee of watch convened to compare all their notes, all they had to conclude was "Amalthea eats grass and a tin can or two." So what else was new? All goats did the same. But they tried this procedure of spying from hill once again with the best and most costly state-of-the-art surveillance equipment from town—then twice, and then thrice, and each time came to same pithy conclusion as first time before: "Amalthea eats grass and a tin can or two. Nothing more." Only this time, under the advice of Professor Triggerfoot II, they now knew the labels of the tin cans she ate, and duly noted them down.

The few other goats that they personally knew were not particular at all on what they would graze. They ate this and that and were traded and sold with freedom and ease. They never stayed put and were like nomads who slept where they pleased. One weed patch was same as the other to owners and them. One tent in the desert just like the next. Their milk always tasted the same as all milk. And the cheese? Well, it was just cheese.

But Harlan ignored them, as best as he could, as did Amalthea too. They minded their business and kept to their wonted old ways.

Deep in the heart of his ancestral land was a thickly grown wood that for scores of his people now dead and long gone had been the great center, the fixed point of life. This wood had tall trees that towered like giants of old and sank their roots deep to the bedrock where water ran sweet in underground rivers and seas. They had never seen sharp axe's gleam. Here buried the family in plot that was sheltered by ancestral trees on gentle round hill. Crooked crosses and fieldstones, and marble, and urns, and carved roses and hands pointing upward, all made a jumble familiar and known as their own. Here Harlan came often with Amalthea to graze. But he was only just passing, for the pasture he sought lay much deeper in wood.

At the center of this forest, which itself was the center of his land and the point where his universe turned, was an opening charmed and remote. It was a great green glen the year round, and sheltered from heat, storm, and cold. It was a place hidden off from the world, kept for family's own.

In this secret place, old Harlan would sit and play fiddle just to himself, while Amalthea grazed. In winter, he would build up his fire and the smoke would rise up straight to the sky, and the sky would wheel round him and it, as if his column of smoke held up the blue as a pillar, or was arm of a wheel that the clouds turned around. And here would his father come looking with his cheerful bright eyes, and once in a while if the music would strike the right key, he would dance a soft shuffling jig or a brief buck and wing, and then disappear in a whirlwind of mist. His mama in the bloom of her youth would for seconds swirl her skirts in the turn of a dance, her arms at her sides and her wrists crooking inward to manage the billows of dress as she swirled and she turned, then was gone in the grey. Grandpa with his ancient musical pipe would marshal deft fingers up and down with a dance of his own, to play a few notes, and the notes he would sound traveled eerily as wind over bottles, or down winter chimneys, or in gutters round the eaves of their home.

Others older than Grandpa would also pass by in review, Grandpa's own father and uncles and cousins and kin that he'd never seen, a trooping kind host that would join in a hazy, slow-motion reel on the old hillside like great dancing floor. They'd join in his song and sometimes play chorus of fiddle with him.

The face of this sheltered green asphodel glen was a rough granite one, sharp with its jags and with shards that could cut like the glass. It was straight up and down, with deep flowing Tyger at base, so on it no mortal had ever touched heel or a toe. It was haunted by both night and day with a river mist that covered fair flowers of clearest cerulean blue. There in the rock opened a crevice that shot back pitch dark in the wall, and from there on the right summer days, old Harlan got a breath of cool air and sometimes the notes for his tunes.

For there the worlds past and present came to touch and lock hands. He had never seen inside the cave, for it beetled too high to be trod or be seen from below. Beneath it, here in the glen, he would fiddle to the tune of the Tyger's flow, with his company passing in memory much older than his own, while Amalthea roamed and grazed at her will, as contented as goddess or god. Here, she'd shed her old bony horns that grew brittle and twisted and gnarled. Here, they lay strewn on the ground. The flowers would soon wreathe them in fragrant bright tufts, and claim them in time as their own. She'd grow then her new horns in light of the world. The shed horns were whorled like the swirls of a dress in the dance in its turn, like a great flying staircase or gyre of stone, or a whirl of gold leaves in the path.

From out the old horns spilled the marvelous fruits of the soil. Today they were flowers, both yellow and blue. Last time, they were grapes from the twist and the twire of a vine that circled around them and danced and ran. Before that, they were berries, plump, blue-black, and bright from off arch of their briary canes. Then earlier still, the red running strawberry poured out of the horns its fresh fully ripe bright scarlet fruit. The horns always would fill to the brim and spill over with the object of Harlan's then current desire. They were, indeed, most magical, miraculous cornucopia horns.

As Harlan played on and nodded his head to the travelers swirling and passing in time with his tune, with passers joining in for brief moments to accompany his chorus of song, Amalthea grazed on the flowers in glen and climbed the steep misty face of the crag no mortal had trod, for there the flower of a much deeper hue of mysterious blue, which grew nowhere else, dropped its nectar in great golden drops like the honey from combs.

It was these that she sought, and she'd eat her quick fill. The first rays of the reddening sun that warned of the end of the day signaled Harlan to break off his song and Amalthea to eat her last flower and join him below for their journeying back.

For those who slept there in the mists of the river at the base of the hill would awake with the chill in their bones and no mind for the world left at all. Their souls would be taken in swirls in the mists to blue depths of the cave, to return only then to the living as fleeting players on fiddles or pipes.

So home to the wife and the hearth, to the shed and the stall. Harlan would drowse with tobacco smoke curling his head, while Sally Pat nodded off in a dream of grand-babies a-plenty, and great-grandbabies to come. Amalthea would sleep on her hooves in her dry tidy stall—on her surefooted hooves that knew well the soil and had climbed where no mortal had been. There on new fragrant hay, she dreamed of the bluest of flowers dripping great honey-dew so sweet to her eager searching goat tongue, while the notes from the cave soothed, fed and enriched, and gentled them all.

Thus Amalthea kept her secret from the strenuous, jet-setting Triggerfoot world, that never had clue, and, loving fads as it did, soon found another fleeting enthusiasm to fill for a time its feverish void.

XXV

Goat Island, a Tale from the Land

When Cousin Shorty was a baby, they'd all done give him up for dead. He ain't called Shorty for no reason, for puny he's always been. He was more than short as a child; it was only short that he got when he grew to be a man. Had to grow up to be short, you'd might say, and that was for a long time in doubt. As a babe, he didn't even have the energy to cry or shake in the cold. Now his pap and mam were poorer even than us, and we was not looked on as kings.

So the doctor, he came on his call and shook his old grizzled head. Shorty'd not last out the month, so puny he was. His mam and pap cussed, cried, prayed, and swore, but mostly looked on pathetic in their worn-out, tired way with that deer-in-the-headlight look so common to them. When old Doc came with his black leather bag, five big-eyed chaps in long shirt tails peered out from behind a table that was empty most time. Life was a struggle and not meant to be fun. They'd sharecropped and tried, and share-cropped some more, but now they'd got whipped and were mostly resigned that this was to be their life and their way. Even the looks of the poor old animals on the place said the same. The worn-out old mule told the tale with its poking-out ribs clearly displayed to the view like they'd cut through the skin. The hounds were so poor they had to lean on a tree just to bark.

Old Doc held out one slim chance for the small baby life. If he could drink the rich milk of a fat nanny goat, and drink to fill up his belly at least three times a day, he might have the chance to see his second birthday. But then Doc shut his bag and the door and the clop of his horse told them all he was gone.

They didn't have no goats. Mam and Pap looked into the room's shadows and sat and sat long, as if searching one out in the corners and empty dark cabinets and shelves. Following lead, their children did too in their big-eyed, hollow-cheeked way. But no goat appeared. Their cousins down the road—that is, us—may would know. Our pap had grit and could do. Yes, and he would. He said that he knew an old man further on down the road, who kept goats on an island way out in a wide stretch of the river that looked like a lake. He said he would ask. The island was full of their kind. They tended themselves, ate on their own, could not wander away. There in their Eden, big dogs could not harm either them or their kids. The billies were kings of the land. The nannies were fat and content with the richness of green. They had prospered and filled up the island in just a few years. Their owner said, "Shore. I got plenty to spare. Go get you the pick of the nannies that's giving good milk."

And he did. But how to get that goat off the island that never had bridge? As usual, Shorty's pap had no plan and trusted our pap to figure one out. Our pap borrowed a leaky old boat that was small in the seat, but could be rowed by a pair. So he set out with Shorty's own pap and, between rowing and bailing, they made it to shore.

They rounded one of the best nannies up, and our pap had to note the fun of the scene, with Shorty's own shiftless dad a-grabbing the goat by the neck and grappling and wrestling to ground. Pap had to keep down a laugh. Even funnier, then, was to see two men rowing and bailing with a fat nanny goat, frozen like statue with shock, seated between.

Our pap did the work, you can be sure. But his brother was a good goat-grappler and holder. We give credit where credit is due.

So there was the trio—the pair and the goat—in silhouette 'gainst the big orange sun as it sank in the stream. But Pap, brother, and goat, unlike sun, did not sink, and made it safe back to shore. It had taken all day.

Yes, the nanny was in shock, as was surely our pap. What a day. His brother, it seemed, had gone nowhere at all, seen nothing that's new. It had happened like breathing, had not ruffled his way, had not made a wrinkle on his ever smooth brain.

Shorty survived, and you see him today. He's a runt, but alive, and is that for the trip to Goat Island way out in the river where the ripe, heavy sun sinks in its bowl of the west, like plump strawberry in newly skimmed cream. The goats frisk on merrily there, not like lambs just exactly, but reasonably close, and the nannies grow fat and content from the green, while the billies still bleat loud as trumpeting horns and lord it like kings.

XXVI
Roses in Snow

In a rare phase, the teller of tales put by his bard's staff and spoke as his own—hard moment of truth with no mask of distance, no guise, from no country behind waterfalls, no land out of mist. It was his own raw place and time. His story ran:

The day after my father was buried, it snowed. Snow was rare enough in our town, especially near Easter, and the event lent a strangeness that death had already given to these unsettled days. The wind flip-flapped the funeral tent, and the hot-house floral wreaths looked as if they were hunkered down shivering. Snowflakes fell on the red rosebuds of his sister, my aunt's, heart-shaped wreath, blown swiftly there with a west wind under the funeral tent. I took the long-stemmed ones from the cluster at the center of the heart into the shelter of the car, his car, and then on into the town, leaving the crooked crosses and carved granite slabs of our country churchyard behind.

The little grey town was starker with the snow coming

down into wet streets. Life was going on in its usual unhurried way. I had to see to some business, tying up loose ends for my mother, little errands occasioned by events.

I walked the sidewalks quickly, as almost in a dream, forgetting my hat, led by impulse and instinct, a reaction to trauma of loss. The flakes tapped softly.

The two gentle women at the bank where my father enjoyed doing his small business were at their usual places—one at the counter, the other at the drive-through. There they sat, as was their custom, back to back, in their measured rhythmical pace of efficient work and conversation. They focused on the tallies, deposits, the counting of cash, in just the intent way they fixed upon the people they served. My father, nearing eighty, had called one of them his sweetheart. The kindness that flowed between them was more rule than exception in the place.

My motions this day were near automatic. With no thinking, from its bunch, I gave her a rose. It may have seemed an odd thing to do, but who was considering? The response was the right one, and the day passed.

On to the service-station around the corner to pay a last bill my father had left in his final weeks. Heads raised to see his car, its presence causing the accustomed viewers lined against the station wall to look up, getting used to the fact that the usual driver no longer drove.

Three of my father's friends since boyhood, all his age, were sitting by the heater in the filling station "office." It was natural to take a seat with them and look out through the plateglass window down to the small intersection that was the town's center.

One of the three was our distant kinsman, who had had a life of some hard knocks and too much drinking. He'd known my father very well as a young man, about the time he married and I was born. With ease, he began to create vignettes of my father, brief stories that flowed as effortlessly as a stream. All were from that time when I was not born, and he knew I would not know them. These came as a gift, a kind of offering to a friend through his son, who would maintain memory through passing the story along.

One tale was of a father I was a little surprised to know. He told of a daredevil nature, an adventuresome one. As steady and serious as I knew him, this side was altogether new, though I was oddly not surprised at it. With the strangeness of snowy landscape, and benumbed by loss, little would have surprised.

He was courting and had a car, whether borrowed or his own, I cannot say. He liked playing the dangerous little game of beating the CNL at the railroad crossing just down our view from the plateglass behind which we sat and looked as the snow fell now more soundly. We joked in our town that the CNL, the official Columbia, Newberry, and Laurens Railroad, stood for the Crooked, Noisy, and Late; but it was not slow.

My father would rev up, gauge his distance, and cross tracks at the last possible moment. This was a game and kept him alert. He liked doing it just for the hell of the thing. And then it was World War II, and that sort of exhilaration from danger must have been in the air.

It all seemed suddenly from another life—in a different land.

When change comes to rooted lives in real places, changes wrought by death and disasters, weddings and births, breaking-ups and comings-together, the way with us is always to talk. I guess the talk is to try to make sense of things, get a handle on change, to ease into the meaning of these losses and gains and adjustments—like crediting why it was no longer my father driving his car or settling bills or sitting there at the window, back against the wall, in the circle of neighbors and friends.

So the ritual was being reenacted before me, and partly for me, and now included me. For the most, I did as I should and kept silence, running on automatic again as the bright snow fell into the wet grey, taking it all in, assimilating, soaking, like the snow dissolving into the warm wet of sidewalks and dark streets.

The talk took the form of stories, as it always does, and the stories put us in mind of ourselves, putting tiny brush strokes of light onto the dark wall of mystery of where we were and who we were, where we were going and why. It all had the solemnness of ballads, the holiness of cathedral chants in ritual, the seriousness that the occasion deserved. And the pauses in our talk were like the refrains in fine old songs, of the angelus and evensong.

Indeed, the talk came in the form of stories, and stories

that made as much sense of things as could possibly be. And strangely, through their filling in of details in the portrait of the young man I could never know, the mystery was deepened, appropriately and starkly. How well do we know anyone, even those closest to us, those even sharing our blood most closely. This did not, and does not, have the effect of unsettling us, for our understanding is that life, that death, are never to be riddled or fathomed or explained.

On this afternoon, then, we sat, and some remembered to others who could not, and, in effect, shared in celebrating the mystery we could never know, and felt bonded in time in this, as we watched the life of the town, our home, acted out in dumb mummer's-show-pageant before us.

Things go well here, as well as they can anywhere, where people have shared the knowing of the world that has gone before them, and that they all have inherited, and will in turn bequeath. People remember, and memories help make sense of the flux we share in swirl. Birth comes to all, joy, satisfaction, loss, grief, death.

I had given one of my father's red rosebuds to his young friend at the bank window just before, and just round the corner; and now the many roses of remembrance were coming back in full open bloom to my father through me, and including me.

That night I dreamed that my father had become me. I sat bolt upright in the bed in tear-wet quilts, in the deep of night, as he was laughing and laughing, as if the joke of his death were really on all of us. He was amused that we thought he had gone, that death had translated him away. The laughter was tinged almost with a kind of sardonic triumph, as he made known that indeed the joke was on me particularly, that he had gone nowhere at all, that he had now instead become me, the father's only son.

I understood clearly then why my numb actions that day in the snow seemed automatic, not my own, why I walked with feet not my own, and gave and received with a self not totally mine.

The montage of these days was deep mystery of mysteries, like red roses full able to blossom in snow.

XXVII
Transistorized Resurrection

Old Uncle Henry and Aunt Sara Bess were quite a pair. They were one, if any two could be. We nephews and cousins down the road always marveled at their old-fashioned ways despite attempts to be up with the times. In this last, they were one as well. Christmas and birthdays, they would always exchange gifts of gadgets, gadgets galore. It would be Salad Shooters for anniversaries, Veg-o-matics under the shiny aluminum tree—and other such of the most useless inventions of all times. It would be clap-on, clap-off lamps for Christmases, so that you found them all over the house. Uncle Henry gave clap-ons to Aunt Bess, and she to him. You couldn't make any sudden moves in any room without it either going dark or startlingly electrifying the place. What with our hand-clapping expressions of delight or surprise, this happened often enough that, when at Uncle Henry's, we learned to tone it down, and be on our guard. This always had the effect of making us self-conscious, never free at our ease.

Their great pastime in the afternoons was watching the shopping channel on TV and finding the damn most useless, climb-a-pole contraptions the Yankee-peddler mind could invent to separate gullible souls from their coin.

Beyond her addiction to gadgets, Aunt Bess had one main vice—a vice she no doubt got from watching so much TV. It must have come from TV, we reasoned, because none of us around her, and not even Uncle Henry, imbibed, except for little glasses of homemade scuppernong wine at Christmas time. He would, of course, on occasion, raise his own Bud, to show solidarity, but he confessed to several of us several times that he hated the stuff—the bitterness set his teeth on edge. So there would sit Aunt Bess in her motorized La-Z-Boy with a fresh, pop-topped cold one at her side, one hand on the chair control and the other on her remote, flipping the thousands of channels of her satellite-dish-fed TV while Uncle Henry sat right up close beside her in his matching motorized chair, with a flat, warm Bud Lite in his hand, held so long his elbow tingled and his arm had grown numb. As they sat side by side, they would clap the lights on every night when it fell dark, and clap the lights off upon going to bed.

And their bed! It did everything for them. It elevated, let down, massaged, shook, and did roller-coaster tricks under the sheets. It heated them in winter with only the flick of a switch and the turn of a dial control. It cooled them in summer with coils. The electrical cords hanging from them as they slept looked like vines in a rainforest, or patients on crucial life supports.

Their kitchen was a real work of art. Cheap Cuisinarts, miniature microwaves, coffee makers (they drew the line at cappuccino machines), electronic choppers, dicers, graters, grinders, mixers, blenders, strainers, freezers, beaters, folders, toasters, roasters, sharpeners, electric knives, can openers, corn poppers, the list could go on and on. To us down the road, we always felt that it was as if the shopping channel from off the TV had exploded, sending its mushroom cloud of fall-out harum-scarum to settle in a jumble lethally all over the room. Funny thing, we thought, Aunt Bess never used the stuff. Truth to say, she wasn't much of a cook. She once made a casserole whose fumes set off the smoke detectors and turned on the clapped-off lights. Ole Cousin Fred across the road solemnly swore they sent his radon gauge screaming into red and made an old Geiger counter click that hadn't for years. They ate TV dinners and Lean Cuisines. She'd peel back the foil, get her a Bud Lite, and call to Henry: "Soup's on." But there was no soup! She had just heard that on ads, as well, on TV. The steam from the little plastic microwave trays would seem to delight their tickled noses as they sat in their La-Z-Boys and surfed the flickering screen.

Well, all good things must come to an end. And so it did with this pair. One morning Aunt Bess didn't rise from the bed and adjust her controls. She'd died of heart failure sometime in the night. The doctor had warned her of being so much overweight and eating just all those junk foods.

Uncle Henry took it in stride, in his patient, stalwart way, and with us made the plans for her funeral. Now Aunt Bess loved one thing even more than Bud Lites, and that was Willie Nelson. She had tape after tape of his songs for her cassette-playing machines. Both machines and his tapes were scattered all over the rooms. She had every song he'd made, in at least triplicate, wherever she went. So it did not surprise us at all that, when we helped Uncle Henry with the funeral plans, he'd insisted on only one thing. The hymns and the casket, preacher, time and the day, these seemed to float by him in a fog, and these we cousins chose and arranged. But the thing he insisted upon, as she lay on the lilac-colored sateen, was to have two things at her side in the casket for her winter's long sleep. The first was a Bud Lite; the second was a pocket transistor that would play cassette tapes. He loaded it up with her favorite Willie high-frequency, extra-long-play. This was done with the undertaker's help, and as it seemed to us all, was natural enough in its way, knowing Uncle Henry and Aunt Bess. What she loved in life, her loved one would want her to have ready at side when she woke.

The echoes of hymns had now gone. The service was over; eyes were wiped dry. The lid of the coffin was fixed down and the pall-bearers bore. Eight hefty shoulders of cousins and kin took her from church on the way to the hill of the cemetery beyond. The crowd, it was large, and followed Aunt Bess in slow, solemn wake. The shoulders, sturdy as they were, had a time with Aunt Bess, for as we have said, she weighed more than her share. So the boys jostled her a bit a few times as they walked on their way. And with one jostle, Aunt Bess must have shifted inside, rolled slightly enough to push her last button control. It was on the cassette-playing machine, for the strains of old Willie came muffled but loud from the box. Uncle Henry had turned the volume as high as it'd go, not knowing how hard it would be to hear on the waking-up day, with all them trumpets and all, as he said, and he'd wanted Aunt Bess to be able to hear. Well, Willie was singing his best at the top of his voice. "On the Road Again." It would have to be that! And sure enough it was, for Aunt Bess. She was on the road all right, with destination unknown.

This, of course, cracked up all us grey-faced followers, even her solemnest closest of kin. Some even laughed loud through their shame. The sturdy pall-bearers, when once they got over their shock, shook casket with mirth, and finally had to set the old dear down, lest she fall. The funeral director had to unscrew the lid and cut off the infernal machine still blaring loud, repeating into Willie's next inspired set. So, procession proceeded and Aunt Bess was duly, solemnly, laid to her rest. But Willie was subject of supper-time stories and was talked of in tales at all country stores, and likely still will be for some time to come.

XXVIII
A Knight of the Sheep

~ ❧ ~

Shepherds and stars are quiet with the hills.
                                    —Vita Sackville-West
. . . a writer's true country . . . what is eternal and
absolute.   —Flannery O'Connor

He was a daydreamer. Most of all, indeed, that's what
he was. Though his face was as wrinkled as the last winter
apple after the frosts, hope showed eternal in his bonny
blue eyes. Often the lambs, urgent for home, would have to
clamber over his sharp bony knees to break him from his
noon apple dreams in the shade. There he would sit, his
back against a tree and his long arms and legs looking like
a great grasshopper on the brink of winter. Sit and sit he
would, as if his hours were seconds, and his minutes days.

He dreamed and he dreamed, eyes open or closed, and
the sheep would graze on. His lonesome ways had become
subject of note in the easy dell where most of us folks in
these parts had our homes and lived out our days. But he
lived on the crest of the hill, where the wind, hill to hill,
blew in gusts that would chill to the bone. We others
sought out the comfortable shelters between.

For all his rough ways, he was our most gentle soul. He
was gentle of voice and gentle of mind. With his crook he

would amble along, humming tunes he made up to himself, and bother no one on his way. He had nothing to spend, nothing to pay. His duty was sheep and he tended them well—from straying, from falls over crags, from an occasional dog or wolf that would kill.

So in gentle amusement, we of the dell had dubbed him The Knight of the Sheep, and all knew his name.

No, as he sat and he dreamed, he'd no sense of time. Yes, the sheep brought him home, and not he them. Why were his hours like seconds, his minutes like days? Why didn't he make segments of time in neat little boxes, either tied up with ribbons of silk, flowered and pinkt, or roped up with twine? We folks in the dell did it one way or t'other, and never demurred—or even for second thought that we might or we may.

Well, for Knight of the Sheep, his time was all memory and hope whose one daughter was art, and he dreamed through the night and the day of this sweet precious child. She was rare as the asphodel meadow in peak of its bloom, or the rose of farthest-sought beauty pinned to the blue of the Blessed Virgin's own blouse, or drifting in petals of pearl from the rose-trellised door of his home.

He thought and he shaped; he dreamed and he mused as he sculpted her marble pure limbs. He dreamed of the silk of the maize for the gold of her hair, and the blue of the gentian or larkspur for eyes. Or then he would make her hair black, with deep pools for her eyes, and the blush of magenta on duskiest cheek.

She changed as he sculpted with dream, but she always returned to fair skin and the shining blue eyes of the gift of his first golden ideal.

We villagers could answer the why and the whereall of that, for The Knight of the Sheep once had such a fair little flesh-and-blood daughter long years ago—that is, measured in their sense of time. And The Knight of the Sheep, in his own, still had her with him on his hill beneath tree.

She had died as a child, taken away in a swirl of the wind on the hill. She had died of a fever, we others would say.

The Knight of the Sheep now had frost in his hair, and his bones and his joints had worn out with his days. He felt as if he creaked when he walked with his staff on the hill. His musings grew deeper and longer with joy of the child.

The day came when his young lambs awoke him no more to go home. They went by themselves to the warm shelter of barn, and The Knight of the Sheep slept out under the cold icy stars, his staff slanting askew on the hard-frozen ground, new-born lamb cradled in arm at his side.

We in the safe valley dell found him there on his wind-swept cold hill, eyes open bright and seated upright, his back to an old rowan tree, like Cuchulainn of yore tied up to a rock fighting waves.

He had witnessed his fair child's return, for he'd sculpted his daughter complete back to life, had finished at last his sweet, arduous chore, and made now of art his little lost child.

XXIX

Orangatan

Neighbor Orangatan was broken from birth. As a child, he wore broken shoes split at the toe, and an old pass-me-down hat broken at the crown. Everything he had always owned had a crack in it. Nothing he achieved was ever whole. Before he could even finish a chore, it needed to be done over. Before he got old Bossy's milk inside, it was like to be spoiled in the pail. Before the crops came in, there would be a bad storm that would flatten the wheat. The day before the harvest, the worms would eat up his corn. Everything he did got almost there, but was damaged or broken or ruined before it was done. So went his life; and with *him,* this is the way it had just always been.

Even his tired old body was broken and bare. The last of the hairs from his balding old head had come out and left his scalp prey to the sun and the cold. His left hip was frozen with pain in the joint, and he had to hibble-hobble on his way. The fingers of his right hand were crippled and drawn, and his back was now stooped with the burden of time and the cares that it brought.

But Orangatan never got bitter, or cursed anyone for his ills, because he kept trust alive in his simple and kindly old heart. He never, like Job, balled up his hand to a fist to complain and to rail. He bore his rough yoke like the unquestioning ox of the field and went on at the plow.

His poor broken wife had worked herself hard and died young. Their children had taken swamp fevers and sickened and nearly all died. The one who survived was broken like him. With no better luck, all things that she tried went awry. But she, like her Pa, always came back for more in her stalwart and hopeful Orangatan way.

He sharecropped as stoically best as he could. He made the place better, grubbing the stumps, removing the rocks, and improving the soil. Then before he could make the good crop that his tendance would yield, there'd come a great drought, or the place would be sold and he'd need a new field full of stumps and of rocks to start over again. So went the waves of Orangatan's unlucky life.

Now the hope of his days, now late in his life, was to make one thing whole, one thing perfect, not broken or marred, leastways mended to be close to perfection some way. Orangatan wanted to do just one thing complete 'fore he died. He set out on his way to complete his often planned journey cross the river to a great shining town he had heard of for all of his days. He'd assembled his bundle and tied it to a stick; but before he could go, his only poor child who survived had her house to catch fire and lost all the pitiful store that she owned. Orangatan stayed with his daughter and helped her rebuild, so put trip to the town far back in his mind. Then the very next month, the poor daughter died.

He next put his mind to polishing a great stone he had found. This stone was a ruby in rough he'd turned up with the point of his plow. In all his spare time, he worked with it, polishing it long and longer than long, to make it a red rose of beauty to eyes that would delight then to see. The rose had begun to glow from inside its prisoned red depths of the stone. It had fires that with patience and time he'd unlocked with his care. But just as he'd needed one final cut, stone cracked into pieces and broke into crumbles of dust. Now he put that aside, like all of the dreams he had had.

But year after year all the time, Orangatan was polishing a thing of great beauty and just didn't know—a thing of even far greater brilliance than ruby in stone. He worked at the labor unknowing with all of his days each time that his great gentle heart made a beat or he drew kindly breath. He'd been given a marred and a broken Orangatan's self, through no particular fault of his own, passed down in the family's Orangatan name. For years through his days, he'd been doing his best, unknown to himself, to complete this one thing, to serve up this object dark ruin could not overtake.

He came to his deathbed in a sharecropper's house that the owner had just sold out from under his tottering feet. The house was to be torn down and carted away, for the making of highway to be. As he lay on his crippled old back all alone, they took him outside to clear way for the wreckers to get on with their job. There on stretcher he died.

But Orangatan in death found at last that the broken was mended, the partial made whole, the unfinished complete, as he yielded up most perfect and clearest bright ruby of all, a soul to the grace of his Maker's own welcoming hands.

L'ENVOI
The Rose of Far-Sought Beauty

A man travels the world over to search for what he needs, and returns home to find it. —George Moore

The teller of tales had grown tired by the hearth and saw that the fire had burned low. The dog that lay on his feet twitched and wrinkled her nose, already in land of dog dreams. The listeners drew closer to share the last warmth of the sputtering coals, which breathed alternately crimson and black as the draft from the chimney whispered across. They were emptying their minds for a winter's long sleep, but begged for some words as a parting to take to the dark and the cold of their quilt-heavy beds.

The tale-teller complied, but the words from his teeming, tired brain passed his lips as a jumble of images ragged and bare like the branches of lightning-struck tree. Yet he struggled to ravel them out through his drowse and fatigue. Half-asleep as he sat, he lay them in tatters like frayed pennons of battle, before neighbors and friends encircling the fire.

From struggle hard fought as they came, they issued in trance of half-sleep in a telling that was gentle and perfect, simple and pure as a dream. They dealt then with yearning and hunger, and

a world past the great heavy bars science keeps, past the gates made of horn and the pearl that open to long winter dreams.

Through gates of the horn grew gentian and lilies, pure Lilies of Truth, grown high in the heart of the rock, seen from afar through mists of the waterfalls plunging to grey smoky rivers and shadowy eddies and pools. But through gates of the pearl lay the rose, the most perfect and pure, the most beautiful rose of the dream. At moments the flower took the form of fair face or shape of a heart, at others, the shining great open face of a book or a beaming bright babe, or the burnished great shield of a knight. At one time it made with its stem the gleaming broadsword, and its thorns, the battlemented wall. Or then it was fire-lit circle of hearth, the carmine of lips, or the jewel-encrusted gold cup and bowl. It was pool and the hilltop, round top of the roof tree, or knoll and the stream. It was misty green shadowy glen in dark Titan wood and merged with the ruby-red clay of the switch-broom-swept yard.

Its petals came in bright saffron dream and dissolved to the red of a sunset's deep glow. It was luminous clear in a morning's bright face, tinged with the pink like the inside of shell, or shone like the rainbow from amethyst scales of a great amber fish, or the rainbow of dancing bright droplets of water it splashed from its watery world. It was pearl froth of the wave, tiny thorn bush, or sumac's thick sheltering great orange crown as the leaves burst suddenly to chorus of song. It was trance in the day, round voice in the patines of blood, or dream in the deep midnight glade.

It was sought far and wide by those wandering feet that never found resting place here upon earth, yearned for by many, both old and the young, through lids open or closed. And it was found by tired seeker most surely at last on its own thorny stem, humbly pinned over heart to the face of a blouse, a rose freshly picked from the trellis at steps of the door of the home of the sleeper's own birth, in the dooryard of home, by the firm-stationed chimney, at the deep-rooted tree at the eave.

Notes

~ ❧ ~

"Child to the Waters" is a phrase from William Butler Yeats' poem "The Stolen Child."

"The Night Her Portrait Sang":

The tale of a singing portrait has been passed down for a century in the Tyger River valley of Upcountry South Carolina. The legend of the benevolent angel of the house who appears at the death of a family member has followed the Hardys of Tyger River from the old world to the new and can be found in the WPA Interviews for Newberry County, South Carolina. In this chapter, several tales and interviews have been interwoven with new narrative.

"Da" and "Dave":

"Da" is the Lowcountry South Carolina term for "nanny" or "mammy." Parts of both of these chapters were inspired by the WPA narratives of former slaves of the Tyger River valley.

"Shone and the Whispering Bridge":

The tale of the whispering bridge, an actual structure, today called Brazelman's Bridge, is locally remembered in Newberry and Union counties, South Carolina. The story usually involves the sighing or crying of a child, heard while crossing the bridge, and the alertness of animals in detecting spirits. From ancient times, trolls and bridges have been a source of fascination. All else in this chapter is invention. The iron skeleton of the old wooden-framed bridge and its massive stone piers are still to be seen off Brazelman's Bridge Road in Newberry County.

"Sad Conacher at Gordon's Mill":

The stone pier ruins of Gordon's Old Bridge, built around 1800, still stand on the Tyger on the Newberry-Union county line.

"Quar":

Mazen Prysock was a locally famous furniture maker and worker in wood in the Stoney Hill section of Newberry County around 1890-1920. He sold his wares in the rural byways by wagon and had something of the reputation among his neighbors as here described. Elements of this story have come down through family narrative. Deirdre comes out of Irish legend, but to different purpose and ends. The ballad "The Bright Sunny South" is a wonderful old one, as is the

206

turn-of-the-century Irish song,"Eileen Aroon," known in various folk versions.

"Singin' Billy, the Song Catcher":

A song catcher in the traditional South is one who collects songs from the people. William Walker, known as "Singin' Billy," to distinguish him from two other William Walkers of the area known as "Hog Billy" and "Pig Billy," was collector and composer of early tunes in his famous *Southern Harmony,* published in Spartanburg, South Carolina in 1835. "Singin' Billy" was born on Padgett's Creek, Tyger River, in 1809. He set in musical notation many of the songs of his day, including old tunes from his mother, and thus ensured their preservation. Some are folk-hymn variants of Scots-Irish reels. As master of various singing schools, he spread sacred music through the South and Old Southwest. Donald Davidson's folk-opera *Singin' Billy* is an excellent mythic treatment of his life and work. Walker died in 1875, after devoted Confederate service.

"The Wee One's Alphabet Blocks":

This occurrence happened to the author at Hardy Plantation on Tyger. The blocks are still with the family.

"How Jakob Emig Encountered Old Scratch":

Using tales are still current now after nearly three centuries in the Dutch (*Deutsch* or German) Fork section of Newberry and Lexington counties, South Carolina. These anecdotes, molded together, are here given a war setting. The stories of the foraging methods of Generals Judson Kilpatrick and Sherman come from diaries, letters, and oral narratives from the area. The "Emig" name is the old German spelling for the present-day Amick family of Newberry and Lexington.

"Dolphus and the Balking Mule":

The basis of this chapter is an old Celtic folk story still in circulation in Eire.

"Croton Oil":

The original narrator of this anecdote is himself famous for taletelling at his country store on Broad River in Fairfield County, South Carolina. He told several of us this story some years ago at his potbellied stove one winter day.

"Fair Grace by the Eddying Pool":

The text of "Bobry Allen," a new world variant of the venerable British ballad "Barbara Allen," comes from a ragged manuscript found by the author in John Taylor family papers of Prosperity, Newberry County, South Carolina. It appears to be from around 1890-1900. Two similar variant texts of the ballad, one sung by Minnie Floyd of Murrells Inlet, South Carolina in 1937, and recorded by John A. Lomax for the Library of Congress, and "Bobree Allin," collected by Reed Smith of Greenville, South Carolina in 1913, are recorded in *Folk Song in South Carolina,* edited by Charles Joyner in 1971.

"Spindleshanks at Ballylee":

The idea of a miraculous singing bush comes from an old Irish legend. Still today in Eire a part of ancient ritual is to walk, dance, or march around a bush in a circle east to west to follow the movements of the sun. This ritual likely originated in Druidic lore, wherein the nether or spirit world is thought to be in close communication with the world of men.

"The Cure":

The story of the wagon burial comes from an old anecdote originating in eastern Greenwood County, South Carolina.

"Sídhe and Ingus":

The ballad "I Left My Dear Father" (like "Bobry Allen") is from a Taylor family manuscript written around 1900 and found by the author in Prosperity, South Carolina. It bears some lines in common with the famous "On Top of Old Smokey" and "A Maid of Constant Sorrow." The great flood of 1863 on the Broad River in Union County provides the inspiration for this story. The stones of prehistoric Fish-Dam Ford rest in the Broad near the hamlet of Carlisle, South Carolina and can be seen when the river is low.

"The Golden Cup and Bowl":

See William Butler Yeats' *Cathleen Ni Houlihan.*

"Amalthea's Horn":

Amalthea's horn of plenty is also known as the cornucopia, ancient symbol of nature's fruitfulness. The Tyger, in its lower reaches, does indeed have such a high rock escarpment and cave. The blue flower, *die blaue Blume,* was a great symbol of Romantic imagination and inspiration.

"Goat Island, a Tale from the Land":

This story is based on oral Connelly family narrative in Newberry County, South Carolina.

"Transistorized Resurrection":

The oral genesis of this tale is reputed to be an actual occurrence in the industrial piedmont of North Carolina.